60 DAY DEVOTIONAL

Walking in Obedience

Learning to Trust God Each Step of the Way

by
Kaysian C. Gordon

Printed in the United States of America

Author photo credit: David Frances Photography

Cover & Interior Design: Watersprings Media House, LLC., www.waterspringsmedia.com

ISBN 13: 978-0-578-74378-3

Dedication

For: Mom, Dad and Amelia

Thank you to everyone who has encouraged me along the way, and shared in this ministry.

Table of Contents

Introduction...1

DAY 1   Walking In Obedience 3

DAY 2   Hold On! Change Is Coming!.............................6

DAY 3   Kindness Begets Kindness 8

DAY 4   My Orchid 11

DAY 5   I Want You To Trust Me 14

DAY 6   Listen... Then Act! 16

DAY 7   Don't Rush The Days Away 19

DAY 8   A God Who Sees Our Needs – And Wants..........22

DAY 9   What Is Your Storm? 25

DAY 10   Sowing Investment Seeds................................28

DAY 11   What Is Your Purpose?.....................................31

DAY 12   What Are You Praying For? 33

DAY 13   My Prayer Journal...36

DAY 14   Be Still And Know..39

DAY 15   He Knows My Name 42

DAY 16   Press The Reset Button 45

DAY 17   Childlike Faith..48

DAY 18   Promises Kept 50

DAY 19   Divine Appointments 52

DAY 20   Questioning God?..55

DAY 21   The Desires Of Our Hearts 58

DAY 22   Partial Truth 61

DAY 23   Holding Hands 64

DAY 24   Spending Uninterrupted Time 66

DAY 25   You Are Loved! 68

DAY 26   In The Fullness Of Time 71

DAY 27   Would You Have Stopped? 73

DAY 28   Are You Preparing? 76

DAY 29   A Changing Season 78

DAY 30   Give Thanks 80

DAY 31   Our Expectations 83

DAY 32   Our Disappointments 86

DAY 33   Distractions 89

DAY 34   I See No Train Traffic 92

DAY 35   God Can Handle Our Honesty 94

DAY 36   Directions 97

DAY 37   Cast Your Cares 99

DAY 38   Shortcut 102

DAY 39   Do You Have The Right Tools? 105

DAY 40   Will You Say "Yes"? 108

DAY 41   Change Your Perspective 111

DAY 42   Worship While You Wait 114

DAY 43   Standing Your Ground 117

DAY 44   Negative Self-Talk 120

DAY 45   My Bruised Thumb 123

DAY 46 Time...126

DAY 47 God Can Change Your Situation In An Instant ...129

DAY 48 God Vs Alexa..132

DAY 49 Listening To Foolish Advice.............................134

DAY 50 Being Loved And Seen......................................137

DAY 51 Are You In Deep Waters?..................................140

DAY 52 Connecting To Jesus...142

DAY 53 Wisdom...144

DAY 54 What You Need.
Where And When You Need It.........................147

DAY 55 Keep Pressing On...150

DAY 56 God's Promises...152

DAY 57 Just Do It!..154

DAY 58 Being Present For Each Other.........................157

DAY 59 Letting Go Of What Holds Us Back 160

DAY 60 Step Out Of The Boat Of Comfort 163

Acknowledgements...166

About The Author...168

Introduction

I'm making final edits to this book in the midst of the Coronavirus, also known as COVID-19. It is a sad time for millions of people who have suffered the loss of loved ones and friends, who have been furloughed or lost their jobs outright, who are facing foreclosure or eviction or who are struggling with the disruption to their normal lives. To be honest, given all that is going on in the world, I did not know whether I would be able to complete it in the time frame that I had set for myself, but alas, by the grace of God, I am marching on.

In February 2019, God laid the title, *Walking in Obedience: Learning to Trust God Each Step of The Way,* on my heart. It seemed a fitting title to follow my first book, *Walking By Faith, and Not By Sight: Learning to Be Still In the Midst of Life's Chaos.* It wasn't until a few weeks into the pandemic that I realized just how apropos the title of my first book was, as God had been teaching me how to slow down the past few years so I could truly hear from Him. However, I must acknowledge that learning to be still in the midst of a pandemic has taken on a whole new meaning. Had it not been for the lessons I learned the first time around; I would not have been able to experience the peace and joy that I'm currently experiencing.

In February 2019, I had a title and a table of contents and was ready to go — until everything got put on hold until just before the fall of that year. Even when my writing resumed, it was a slow process; however, with God's help to keep me focused, I never lost sight of the goal. Just a reminder: "delayed does not mean denied." Yet, even with the book right there in front of me, it still felt far away. I believe God wanted me to have peace and stillness as I put this second book together, but too much was going on in my life as I transitioned from one career path to a new one that God had ordained. After all, it was just too crazy to have been my idea. See, I've read in a number of places that if an idea comes to you that is too crazy for you to have originated, it is a test from God — a test of obedience.

So, what was this crazy idea that God had cooked up for me? Entrepreneurship. Imagine that. A divorced mom of a young child becoming an entrepreneur. Lord knows that would definitely not have been my idea. But when God calls you, He also makes a way out of no way for you to succeed at what He called you to do. Since He called me and I decided to be obedient, my life has been incredibly blessed. I won't tell you there haven't been moments of stress-induced anxiety, because there have. But, even so, I am constantly reminded that when God calls you, He will provide for you.

As I sit here in complete peace, amid the craziness of what is happening in the world, I want to offer you a word of encouragement: If God is calling you out to do something that seems "left field" for you, please confirm that it is indeed Him calling you. Once you confirm that it is God calling you, do not hesitate to move forward. Many of the devotionals in this book are based on a central question or concept: Will you say "yes"? It may be the craziest idea to you, but God has already opened up the paths for you and is waiting for you to take a leap of faith and walk into the paths He has laid. You, however, have to take the first step. Will you join me?

Have I not commanded you? Be strong and courageous. Do not be afraid; do not be discouraged, for the LORD your God will be with you wherever you go.

JOSHUA 1:9 NIV

DAY 1
Walking In Obedience

I met a friend on the train some time ago. I had seen him reading a devotional and interrupted him and gave him my blog card. I felt a little weird doing it, but felt I should. When he was finished, he explained that his mom had given him the book and he was playing "catch up" after missing a few days of reading it for the second time.

We talked about our similar professions, and he said he needed to do some continuing education. Although I had done the continuing education courses and would have liked to share information with him, at that moment I could not remember the course I used. I offered to take his number to text him the info when I got to my desk. Within ten minutes of departing, I remembered the information. But God in His infinite wisdom knew why we needed each other's numbers, as our contact was not to end after only one train conversation.

We have seen each other since. In fact, often when I thought of him I would run into him on the train, which allowed me to check on him.

A few days ago, he reached out to me. God had been calling him for a while, and he knew that God wanted his attention. But that day it was different. He knew he could no longer continue avoiding God and needed to answer Him.

God laid it on his heart to reach out to me. When he reached out, we had the opportunity to pray and talk and as I shared my experiences. We both knew why God led him to me; he needed to start his own faith journey.

He was unsure how to proceed, but within a day I read a devotion that I knew was for him and subsequently shared it with him. It basically reminds us that when God calls us, He equips us to step into our calling. My friend is already putting plans in place for when he gets his initial direction, and I am humbled as I watch the work God is starting.

Please lift him in prayer as he chooses to walk in obedience — no matter how his decision may seem to friends, family and colleagues.

Is God calling you for something that doesn't seem to make sense to you? Believe me when I tell you that He will equip you. Will you say 'yes' to God?

Dear Heavenly Father, thank you for God-ordained friendships. I ask that you be with my friend and those whom you have called. Help them see that when they willingly lose their lives to you, you will give them life more abundantly. Help us to say 'yes' to what you are calling us to do.

But Samuel replied, "What is more pleasing to the LORD: your burnt offerings and sacrifices or your obedience to his voice? Listen! Obedience is better than sacrifice, and submission is better than offering the fat of rams."

1 SAMUEL 15:22, NLT

Thought to ponder

Have you ever been given a set of instructions that do not seem to make sense to you or take you completely out of your comfort zone? What do you do?

____

____

____

____

____

____

____

____

____

____

____

____

____

____

DAY 2

Hold On! Change Is Coming!

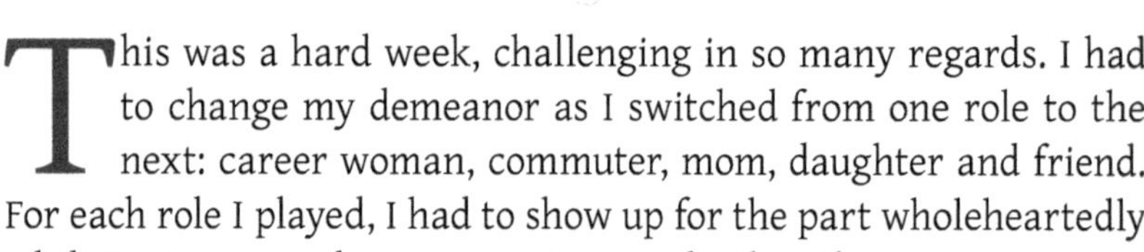

This was a hard week, challenging in so many regards. I had to change my demeanor as I switched from one role to the next: career woman, commuter, mom, daughter and friend. For each role I played, I had to show up for the part wholeheartedly while trying not to let one aspect overtake the other.

During a conversation with a friend, she shared some of her struggles. As I sat listening to and looking at her, all I could think was 'Thank God we don't look like what we've been through.'

For this season I am walking through, I am reminded of what my then future counselor said when I reached out for a consultation… 'No matter how good or bad, this time will soon change.' I have clung to those words for many years. No matter how difficult the season you are walking through, please be reminded that it will change. And if you are in a good season, enjoy it and use the time to strengthen your fortitude for when a not-so-good season hits.

Are you walking in a difficult season? I promise you, it will come to an end. I can look back over so many seasons that I thought would never end. But guess what? I'm not dealing with those issues anymore. In fact, now they are but a distant memory.

Be encouraged. God gives power to the weak. Ask Him.

Dear Heavenly Father, thank you for your grace and for allowing our seasons to change. Thank you for enabling us to have hope in you and for letting us know that we can look forward to brighter days. Help us to learn from our experiences and to share with others so they, too, can be victorious over trials.

He gives strength to the weary and increases the power of the weak.

ISAIAH 40:29, NIV

Thought to ponder

Are you walking through a particularly difficult season for which you cannot see an ending? How can you hold on just a little bit longer?

DAY 3

Kindness Begets Kindness

*It is difficult to give away kindness.
It keeps coming back to you.*
CORT FLINT

For nearly 15 years, that quote has appeared at the end of my emails. It's a simple statement, but one that is packed with truth.

Throughout my life, I have found the more I extend kindness, the more it comes back to me — sort of like a boomerang.

One of my colleagues and I enjoy bananas, which are provided at the beginning of the week in our work pantry. One day I saw a few bananas that were almost perfect, (usually it's hard to get even one that's close) so I grabbed two — one for him and one for me. He was appreciative and made a big show of the banana and the fact I'd gotten it for him.

This friend knows I like flavored seltzer, so the next day he grabbed two from the pantry and proudly handed me one.

I smiled, because the topic of kindness had already been laid on my heart. You see, people who know this colleague know that demonstrating kindness isn't second nature to him.

I'm teaching my daughter about kindness and am thrilled over her understanding. It's not uncommon for her to come home with little stickers proclaiming she's been "caught" being nice to others. Moreover, her class just had their third party to celebrate receiving numerous kindness compliments.

My daughter likes being allowed to wear pajamas to school — which her teacher permitted on the day of the party. I was thrilled when she asked for stationery so she could write a thank you note to her teacher, and equally glad to learn her teacher gave her a hug in return.

I can just picture her teacher's face when she saw the card written as only a six-year-old could. And I have a pretty good sense of how special it made her feel.

Kindness really does beget kindness.

Let us endeavor to share kindness with each other. It really is difficult to give away kindness, as the true recipient may very well be the giver.

> Dear Heavenly Father, sometimes we may get so stuck in our own situations that we become oblivious to those around us who need a kind word or a good deed. Help us to be more mindful of those who are hurting. Help us to extend kindness to them, even when we are in need of a little bit of kindness ourselves. Let random acts of kindness become the "new normal." Help us all to benefit from acts of kindness.

> *Be kind and compassionate to one another, forgiving each other, just as in Christ God forgave you.*
>
> Ephesians 4:32 NIV

Thought to ponder

Is there someone to whom you are struggling to be kind?
How can you change that?

DAY 4

My Orchid

I first started sharing about my Orchid adventures almost three years ago, and would you believe my Orchids have never sprouted flowers in all of that time?

It's a sad but true fact. I've planted tomatoes and flowers and they've grown and flourished, so I know it's not for lack of a "green thumb."

I have iced my Orchids consistently. Nothing. I have changed their pots. Nothing. I have added Orchid potting chips. Nothing.

The only reason I kept doing all of those things is periodically there were signs of life. I remember once getting excited over the sprouting of a new "branch," but after giving it what I thought was careful attention, the pseudo branch withered away. Again. Nothing.

My frustration over consistently watering my Orchids only to get no results tempted me to just tell my mom to take them. I figured may she would have better luck than me, and, admittedly, I knew I'd been less than diligent about icing them. Thoughts of why bother and nothing is happening kept creeping into my mind, yet even so, when I remembered to ice them I halfheartedly did it.

Somehow in the last week, I took the time to actually look at one of the Orchids and realized that a new branch had sprouted! Not only had it sprouted; it had actually grown over three-to-four inches long. All the time I thought my efforts were futile, real progress was being made! I'm still waiting for it to actually flower, but I am encouraged that something is, finally, indeed happening.

Do you feel this way about something — or someone — in your life?

You have seemingly been doing all of the right things, yet you've gotten no visible results of progress or change?

I want to encourage you today to hold on and keep the faith. In fact, I pray that neither you nor I will give up but, instead I pray that we will reap our rewards in the proper time.

Dear Heavenly Father, I am grateful for these lessons. Help me to continue doing the little things that I should do, even when I grow frustrated over the lack of results. Help me to see that these instructions build my character for use in Your Kingdom.

Let us not become weary in doing good, for at the proper time we will reap a harvest if we do not give up.

GALATIANS 6:9 NIV

Thought to ponder

In what area of your life have you been diligently working yet seeing no results? What can you do to keep persevering?

DAY 5
I Want You To Trust Me

Have you ever thought you knew what something meant only to realize you were clueless?

I remember walking home from work on a day when I'd been frustrated over a nagging situation for which I just didn't have an answer. As I walked by Barnes and Noble in Manhattan, near a set of huge potted plants, I asked God, why are You taking me through this situation? The answer came back immediately in a small, almost whisper-like voice, "because I want you to trust Me".

I've pondered that day many times, and the one thing I always come back to is the fact that God wants us to reach out to him for all things — big and small. You see, I've lived a very independent life, doing what I deem the right thing most of the time — actually just some of the time if I'm honest — and asking for God's guidance only on "big" things. I think God was trying to get me to understand that day that He is a father who cares about all of the details — the big ones as well as the minuscule ones.

Since then, I've walked through various seasons. Now that I'm sitting back and revisiting them, I can easily see that God's hands were all over everything I encountered. Likewise, I realize what he meant that day as I walked past Barnes and Noble and he whispered, "because I want you to trust me." I can assure you I'm still reluctant, at times, to leap out on faith and totally trust God. That means, of course, there will be many more instances when He will say to me, "I want you to trust me." I don't believe I can learn how to trust fully, as it's not something we've been taught to do. But God outdoes Himself and expects nothing less than our full and complete trust.

Dear Heavenly Father, thank you for being trustworthy, which You demonstrate time and again. Thank you for allowing us, when we submit to You and walk with You, to more fully understand what trusting you looks like, even when we can't see the outcome or understand the process through which You are taking us.

Trust in the LORD with all your heart and lean not on your own understanding; in all your ways submit to him, and he will make your paths straight.

PROVERBS 3:5-6 NIV

Thought to ponder

What is one area in your life in which you are struggling to trust God? Why do you think you're struggling to let go?

DAY 6

Listen... Then Act!

Have you ever had a sense that you should or shouldn't do something?

One day after finishing lunch in my home office, I decided to temporarily leave my plate on the floor next to me instead of and putting it in the trash can. Even though it was greasy from the vegetables I'd been eating, and though visions of me stepping in the plate flashed through my mind, I disregarded all of that and vowed there was no way I'd absent-mindedly step in the plate. No worries, I thought. I'll put it away soon.

A while later I got a phone call and had to get up. Without a moment's thought I spun around and stepped onto the plate, splattering large patches of green grease on my almost-white carpet. I was annoyed at myself but didn't have time to survey the damage as I needed to tend to something right then. Later, when I went back to clean the carpet with a Clorox wipe, I realized the irony: I could have saved so much time had I just put away the plate away when I initially thought about it.

Later that day I ran into my friend. Our kids had had a play date the day before, and while they were playing, we sat and talked and I learned that her family was preparing for an upcoming trip.

Now she explained that after my daughter and I left, she continued packing for the trip. As she packed, she got a sense that something wasn't right. She couldn't put her finger on it, but something was amiss. When she checked her kids' passports, she discovered they were both expired. There were only four days left before the trip, and only two of them were business days. After researching virtually all night, she was able to get the process started to ensure their new passports arrived in time for their long-awaited family vacation.

Just imagine if she had been like me and ignored her inner thought. It's one thing to have to pay a little bit of money to have carpet cleaned. It's a different ballgame altogether to have to miss out on a family trip — not to mention lose money — because you didn't listen to your hunch that something wasn't right.

I pray that you act accordingly the next time you get a sense that you should or shouldn't do something.

> Dear Heavenly Father, sometimes we do or don't do things that we feel convicted to because we believe they're small and inconsequential. Help us to realize that little things can lead to bigger things. Prick our hearts when we are — or are not — doing things that we should be doing.

The eyes of the LORD are on the righteous, and his ears are attentive to their cry.

PSALM 34:15 NIV

Thought to ponder

Have you ever had a distinct feeling that you should or shouldn't do something, but ignored it? What was the end result?

DAY 7
Don't Rush the Days Away

By now you know how much I love surprising my daughter with different activities. Occasionally I'll tell her what we're doing. At other times I'll tell her only the time special activities will occur. Either way, we make a big deal out of just about everything.

Whenever I make a promise, I bust my butt to execute on it. If I tell my daughter the date of an upcoming activity, she starts counting the days and wishing it was already the day of said event. Sadly, she inherited her mother's impatient nature.

During moments when my daughter gets anxious about a certain event or date, I find myself telling her "don't rush the days away." As it is, she's already growing up way too fast for my liking, so when she says, "I wish it was the day of XYZ already," I chuckle at her impatience and gently tell her to stop wishing the days away.

But, of course, God nudges me in those moments, and I'm sure you can guess what he says. In layman's terms it's an oft-used phrase: the pot calling the kettle black. In Biblical terms, it's more like Matthew 7:5, which says, "Hypocrite! First remove the plank from your own eye, and then you will see clearly to remove the speck from your brother's eye." (NKJV)

Am I not like my impatient daughter? I want God to do some things in my life, and often times I want him to do them "yesterday." Talk about the Queen of Impatience. But God prompts me, just like I do my daughter, and reminds me not to wish the days away and to enjoy the different seasons I'm in, because this is where growth happens.

As I look back over the last several years, I realize had I gotten my quick answer from God I wouldn't be the person I am, nor would I be growing into the person He's molding me to be. When processes are rushed, things usually turn out poorly.

I have recently acquired this saying: a half-baked cake is not edible.

A cake has to stay in the oven at just the right temperature, and for just the right amount of time, to bake successfully. And don't even think about opening the door to check on it — unless you want it to flop. Ask me how I know. That's right. I learned the hard way.

Dear Heavenly Father, thank you for providing humorous, real-life examples of what impatience can do in our lives. Thank you for being an expert baker, potter and silversmith. You know exactly how much time it takes to bake, mold and refine us, and you don't allow anything or anyone "to bake" for one second longer than need be. Help us to not wish the days away as you take us through the process.

Not only so, but we also glory in our sufferings, because we know that suffering produces perseverance; 4perseverance, character; and character, hope. 5And hope does not put us to shame, because God's love has been poured out into our hearts through the Holy Spirit, who has been given to us.

ROMANS 5:3-5 NIV

Thought to ponder

Do you have a tendency to wish the days away when you know something exciting is happening soon? How do you combat your need for rushing the days away?

DAY 8

A God Who Sees Our Needs – and Wants

Have you ever read the stories in 2 Kings 4?

The chapter is broken down into four distinct stories: The Widow's Oil; The Shunammite's Son Restored to Life; Death in the Pot; and Feeding of a Hundred.

I see these stories as evidence of a God who provides for our needs, including those of which we aren't even cognizant.

As my daughter and I were walking in a store a few days ago to purchase our contribution to her class party, she asked for something. Because she hadn't had this particular item in a long time, I gave in and told her she could have it. As we were walking to the cashier, she said, "Mommy, you got what you needed, and I got what I wanted." I smiled inwardly, very impressed that she knew the difference.

Today, I want to discuss the Shunammite woman, who's been described as well-to-do. She had everything she needed, and when Elisha passed through her town during his travels, she'd welcome him and his servant in for a meal. I guess he passed by fairly often because she suggested to her husband that they create a room for him during his stays. (I love her generous spirit.)

After enjoying hospitality at her home several times, Elisha wanted to return the kindness. The only thing she apparently lacked was a child. Given her age, in those days, I assume she probably had tried to have children, to no avail. One day when Elisha told her that in a year she was going to have a son, her words were "No, my Lord... don't mislead your servant, O man of God!"

Notice that even while telling him not to mislead her, she was careful to remind him of just who he was.

Guess what? At the exact time Elisha predicted she would have a son, she did.

There's a lot more to this story, but I want to encourage you and me.

Has God given you a promise that hasn't yet been fulfilled?

Don't lose heart because you think a lot of time has passed. God knows exactly when His promise needs to be fulfilled. Hang on just a little bit longer. Don't be afraid or discouraged.

> Dear Heavenly Father, thank you for being a God who provides, even in situations when we have long since given up hope. I pray that as we experience moments of discouragement You will remind us of Your promises and that You always keep Your word. Help us to be obedient and do what you ask us to do.

> *But the woman became pregnant, and the next year about that same time she gave birth to a son, just as Elisha had told her.*
>
> 2 KINGS 4:17 NIV

Thought to ponder

Are you discouraged about a need you've asked God for that hasn't yet come to fruition? Do you believe this is truly a promise from God?

DAY 9

What is Your Storm?

I've heard Priscilla Shirer say, "You're either in a storm, coming out of one or about to enter one."

What a true statement.

We experienced several nights of rough seas and heavy rains on our last cruise, worse than I remember on previous trips. On the last night, as we all packed and prepared to depart the ship the next day, it rocked so hard that a female passenger said the swaying gave her motion sickness and prevented her from packing.

As an indicator of how bad it was, barf bags were placed around the ship when the rough patch began. On the last night, I felt my body sliding up and down the bed as the ship swayed. I even awakened to the sound of water splashing on my fifth-floor window.

We were in quite a storm, and I began praying as I'd never been on a ship in such extreme weather — not to be mention this was one of the largest ships I'd been on, which means it should have been more stable.

After I prayed I began thinking. I'm in a storm. What am I going to do? Jump overboard because the ship is rocking so badly? Then I remembered the story of when the train goes through the tunnel and finds complete darkness. Do we try to get off the train during the darkest times?

Of course I wasn't going to jump overboard. Nor was I going to jump off a train while riding through a tunnel.

Just like the captain on that cruise ship, we have a Captain who has gone through countless storms. And this Captain even sleeps through storms because He knows who He is and even the winds and seas obey Him.

Friends, storms will always rage in our lives, and I pray that you find the only true anchor to hold you when you feel wave-tossed and thrown about. I pray you don't try to jump ship during uncomfortable situations but instead have faith and rely on God to see you through.

Dear Heavenly Father, we thank you for being a dependable, life-saving anchor. Help us to always trust that truth! Help us to hold onto you with the knowledge that you will never leave us or forsake us — especially during our darkest times. You have promised to be the one to carry us through, but we must trust you and leave our worries in your care.

24 *Suddenly a furious storm came up on the lake, so that the waves swept over the boat. But Jesus was sleeping.* **25** *The disciples went and woke him, saying, "Lord, save us! We're going to drown!"* **26** *He replied, "You of little faith, why are you so afraid?" Then he got up and rebuked the winds and the waves, and it was completely calm.*

MATTHEW 8: 24-26 NIV

Thought to ponder

Can you think of a storm that raged or is currently raging in your life?

DAY 10

Sowing Investment Seeds

I have a very good mommy friend who was out of work for more than eighteen months. God provided for her needs during that time, but she received no paycheck.

One day she texted that she'd started working! I was excited for her and told her I wanted to hear all about how she got the job, as I just love a good story/testimony and knew she had been job hunting for a long time. Moreover, I had been praying for quite some time for God to bless her with a job.

She shared that around Thanksgiving a friend handed her an envelope with $100 in it. Although she definitely could have used the money after being out of work for so long, she felt convicted to give it to her church — so she did.

She said within a week of giving the love offering to her church, she got a call for a temp position with benefits — a rarity for sure! Moreover, in the process God provided care for her daughter so that she didn't miss a beat in getting her to school.

Why am I sharing this particular story?

Sometimes we have to plant investment seeds. As we petition and beg God to do the impossible, especially with our finances, sometimes we have to do things that seem illogical to us. In all my years of returning tithes and offering at church, I've discovered that God's math just doesn't make sense. I've heard many stories from friends who say that when they're faithful with a little, God turns it around and makes it much. Conversely, when we try to hold on to what we deem too tiny an amount to share, the amount we withhold ends up costing us much more.

Remember the widow with the two mites, also known as cents? She was specifically mentioned in the Bible because of her faithfulness. She wasn't wealthy, so unlike the others, she wasn't giving "excess" money she wouldn't miss. Instead, she gave all she had, trusting that her needs would be provided.

I want to have faith like the widow so that I manage my resources and show myself as a good steward.

Dear Heavenly Father, thank you for the resources You provide to take care of our needs. Help us not to try to hold onto every dollar we have, because a closed fist can neither give nor receive. Help us to be obedient to promptings to give to our church and those in need.

1 *As Jesus looked up, he saw the rich putting their gifts into the temple treasury.* **2** *He also saw a poor widow put in two very small copper coins.* **3** *"Truly I tell you,"* *he said, "this poor widow has put in more than all the others.* **4** *All these people gave their gifts out of their wealth; but she out of her poverty put in all she had to live on."*

LUKE 21:1-4 NIV

Thought to ponder

Have you ever felt convicted to share your resources but decided not to? What was the end result?

DAY 11

What is Your Purpose?

Do you ever wonder what purpose some animals or insects serve?

My daughter and I spent our last vacation cruising the high seas, in a ship affiliated with marine biologist Guy Harvey, who designed its hull and has his own tv channel on board. My daughter was fascinated with this channel because it showed under water life and many of the documentaries focused on sharks and ways we can save and protect them.

While I'm fascinated by what lies beneath the surface, I know that the ocean and what's in it are not to be messed with — especially sharks.

From watching several documentaries, I gathered that every fish or animal has a purpose in the circle of life, even corals. If you're wondering what is the purpose of sharks, you and I are in the same boat. While they seem to have a bad reputation and are generally considered killers, Guy Harvey believes they're not what we think and has set up foundations to protect them and other underwater life. There's even a slogan: "Healthy oceans need sharks."

Did you know that each fish, plankton, whale and shark serve their own unique purpose? Each does, which prompted me to wonder whether I'm living out my purpose. Likewise, it made me question whether I even know what my purpose is.

Dear Heavenly Father, thank you for having our purpose in mind even before creating us. Father, sometimes we forget that we are fearfully and wonderfully made and created as unique beings and that no one will ever be able to do the job that You have called us to do. Help us to seek You as we seek to fulfill the purpose for which You have called us.

God said, "I command the ocean to be full of living creatures."
GENESIS 1:20A CEV

Thought to ponder

What do you consider as your purpose?

____

____

____

____

____

____

____

____

____

____

____

DAY 12

What Are You Praying For?

On one of our most recent cruises, my daughter saw a lady and decided she wanted to spend time with her. Given we were all going on the same excursion, I told her it was okay. Another reason I said yes is I know my daughter typically sees in others what most don't. The lady had been traveling with her cousin, but she'd chosen a different excursion so at this point she was alone. Needless to say, she willingly accepted my daughter's invitation to be her "playmate."

The next day, I chose to be more intentional in my prayer after seeing the joy we brought to the lady, and I asked God to lead us to people to whom to show His love.

After getting off the ship, I had planned to take a boat to an island I'd visited before, and that's when I found out I could have only booked the trip through the ship. No worries, I was on an island with many other options.

As I told the taxi service driver where I wanted to go, I was informed I'd have to wait about ten to fifteen minutes. No problem, as I was already on island time. Within two minutes, they called me over and said a taxi headed to where I was going had two spots left. When my daughter and I got in and started talking to the other passengers, one of the dads shared that he and his family were spending the day at a resort on a day pass and I was welcome to join them. I quickly assessed the invitation, decided I didn't have much to lose and decided to go.

Only God could have set that up, as I quickly realized it was the answer to my prayer in reverse. Here were two sets of families who were to be a blessing to my daughter and me. One of the moms shared stories with me as she answered questions that I'd been asking God as to what my next steps were to be. She confirmed everything that had been laid on my heart. She and I cried, had goosebumps and laughed at how God worked.

We spent a lovely day with them before separating to go to our respective ships, as we weren't even on the same cruise.

Sometimes we say prayers not knowing how or whether God will answer them. I say 'or whether' because sometimes we pray to God and ask for things that He knows we don't need. Moreover, I'm learning that He has a way of answering our prayers far better than the way we can think or imagine. The lady I befriended on the excursion spoke blessings over me and what would become my next career move.

Heavenly Father, thank you for being a God who hears and answers our prayers, and thank you for answering in ways that far exceed our thoughts. Thank you for sending strangers to walk us through situations or questions that we face. Father, make our hearts receptive to hearing in the different ways you choose to speak.

For the word of God is alive and active. Sharper than any double-edged sword, it penetrates even to dividing soul and spirit, joints and marrow; it judges the thoughts and attitudes of the heart.

HEBREWS 4:12 NIV

Thought to ponder

What are you asking God for? Are you receptive to the different ways He speaks to you, whether it's through others or His Word?

DAY 13

My Prayer Journal

At the beginning of the year, a close girlfriend reached out to ask if I wanted to participate in a forty-day prayer challenge with her. Admittedly, I was a bit skeptical. I am selfish with my quiet time and really prefer to go it alone. However, as I had been goal setting the week before and one of my goals was to pray more, I decided that engaging in consistent prayer with someone who already knew so much about me might help me achieve that goal.

So I said yes and tried to recruit a few more friends to join in. No one accepted.

I found out later that my girlfriend had actually been reluctant to ask me because she knew I was busy. Likewise, I learned that she had also tried, in vain, to recruit a few of her close friends and family.

My friend and I were in this together. In the words of Bill Withers — just the two of us.

As a part of this forty-day challenge, I wanted to ensure that I wouldn't just read the book but also be an active participant by writing down the lessons I learned daily. I encouraged her to do the same and suggested she get a prayer journal, as I just love writing in mine. I even told her to make sure she prayed before going to purchase her journal. Over the years I've discovered there's just something beautiful about writing down your thoughts to go back and read later.

I have been given a few journals as gifts in the last couple of years. I even used one I bought as my client notebook because of the scriptural encouragement each day provides. I had bought a new one months before, which had 2 Corinthians 5:7 on the front, "I will walk by faith even when I cannot see." I was literally using the last few pages of my current journal and looking forward to starting my new crisp journal/notebook — until I sensed God telling me to give it to my friend.

But God...I've had this prayer journal for months, and I'm really looking forward to using it now. And not only that, it's going to double as my new notebook.

The next day while attending a work-related luncheon, I received a brand-new notebook with my company's logo on the front.

I knew I was out of excuses.

I called my friend and told her she no longer had to go searching for the "right" prayer journal as I had one for her.

I also told her my dilemma and that I was giving it to her reluctantly but in obedience with what God had told me to do. She knows me well enough to know that I'll be honest. In fact, we both laughed over it.

My obedience has turned into a huge blessing for her because it has shown her that God cares about even the smallest details of her life. Ironically, her phone screen message says she is walking in a season of complete faith. As we prepared to continue our forty-day prayer challenge, she teased me about writing in her beautiful journal that her good friend gifted to her.

Dear Heavenly Father, sometimes we don't understand the impact that our simple obedience will have on someone else. Help me to always be quick to obey, even if what You're telling me to do isn't what I originally had in mind as I'll never quite grasp the work that You are doing in someone else's life.

Now faith is confidence in what we hope for and assurance about what we do not see.
HEBREWS 11:1 NIV

Thought to ponder

Is there something God has asked you to do that you are reluctant to execute? In what ways are you being prompted to obey?

DAY 14

Be Still And Know...

I write a weekly blog, and if by Thursday it's not clear to me what the message should be, I start praying even harder for the topic. When I first started writing, I used to get worried when I didn't know what my topic was, but now I trust God to give me just the right topic that that one person needs to hear.

I like to be in control of my life. Name an independent woman who doesn't? But God has other plans for my life and wants to be in total control of everything. While you and I might think it's great to allow God to be in total control, the truth is it's a bit — frankly a lot — uncomfortable for me. That's because I'm used to thinking I have everything under control — until God steps in and reveals something entirely different

I'm used to coming and going as I please and doing what I want. I went to God with a specific request, and instead of answering it out right, He said to my heart "Be still and know that I am God... Is there anything too hard for me to do?"

Since then, He has used the last few years to transform my life. He's taken a non-author, non-speaking private person and converted me into a published author, speaker and one who shares willingly and excitedly about things I once held very private.

When we cry out to God to intervene in a situation, He may not answer right away or in the way we expect. Instead, He'll come alongside and transform us from the inside out. He might say to you "My grace is sufficient for you," or He might say to you, 'I know it's hard, but just hang on to Me a little tighter, and we'll get through this together." He also might say to you, "This is how you'll see My everlasting love for you during these hard situations."

What difficult situation are you facing this morning?

God is reminding me, "Be still and know that I am God." What is He telling you?

Dear Heavenly Father, You know the message we each need to hear that will settle our hearts as we learn to trust You. I pray you'll show each person who's going through a difficult season or a difficult decision right now Your unfailing love and how You've been there all along. We thank You for Your everlasting love.

He says, "Be still, and know that I am God; I will be exalted among the nations, I will be exalted in the earth."

PSALM 46:10 NIV

Thought to ponder

What is the difficult situation you're facing that keeps you hanging onto God's promises? What is He telling you about this particular thing?

DAY 15

He Knows My Name

One particular weekend I was having a difficult, emotional time.

I went to church and heard a great sermon on faith, but my heart just didn't seem receptive to the message. Has that ever happened to you? You know that God is reminding you that He is in the midst of everything and nothing happens without His permission, but you just still have a "woe is me attitude". Well, that was me — for days on end.

I've also stopped giving those I know love and care for me the pat answer of "I'm ok" when I'm not. Instead, I'm forthright and articulate my feelings when asked what's wrong. Sometimes I have to think a little bit harder to really process what's going on and why, in a certain moment if I'm not feeling okay.

Thankfully, when I'm truthful about how I'm feeling with my friends, I don't receive cliché responses. One friend texted "I understand" with an avatar of himself shedding a tear, which conveyed that he understood. Another friend called me by a name that only we understand and told me she was praying for me, which I didn't doubt for a second.

I kept hearing a song repeated in my head, and typically when that happens I go to YouTube and find it. I did that this time and listened to the song. When it ended, "He Knows My Name" by Tasha Cobbs automatically started playing. That song, though beautiful, isn't in my usual playlist, but I've often thought YouTube "has a mind of its own" when it comes to playing music. Not only did it play, automatically, but it played three different times in three different versions, back-to-back-to-back. There's no doubt that this was a stark reminder to me that God knows my name and everything about me. Despite how I was feeling and the "woe is me" mentality that had tried to take over, God had not forgotten me.

When I awoke the next morning, there was a devotion on Proverbs 31.org (I visit this site daily) on the very topic with which I'd struggled the last few days. Ironically, it even referenced some of the emotions I'd been feeling.

Now to whom could I attribute that but God? He was reminding me that I hadn't been forgotten and was deeply loved.

Whenever you're going through a difficult time, please be reminded that He knows your name and you are not forgotten. Seek friends and family who will comfort you and be there for you in practical ways.

Dear Heavenly Father, thank you for knowing me by name and for not letting anything happen to me without Your permission. You're the author and finisher of my faith, and I need to trust only You and Your plans for my life.

But now, this is what the LORD says – he who created you, O Jacob, he who formed you, O Israel: "Fear not, for I have redeemed you; I have summoned you by name; you are mine."

ISAIAH 43:1 NIV

Thought to ponder

Do you really believe God knows you by name, as well as all of the circumstances you're facing? Why or why not?

DAY 16

Press The Reset Button

I've had many good, even great things happen in my life. I'm a career woman, a mom, a published author and wear many other hats... See? Lots of good things. Except each of those good things has been pulling me in a different direction.

I'd gotten to the point of being on empty but characteristically kept pushing and continued going until one day my body retaliated and said 'no more.'

My brain wasn't processing things the way it usually did. I was easily distracted and couldn't remember the task at hand from one moment to the next. I was more easily irritated. And, finally, I was quiet. If you know me, you know that it's not a good sign when I'm quiet. Moreover, I hadn't been quiet for quite some time.

The day my body said no more, I decided to do something I rarely do. I stayed home, put the phone in 'do-not-disturb' mode, didn't tell anyone I was home, and I slept.

Rest. Why is it that we often get to the point of complete exhaustion before we realize we need to rest?

We're all capable of doing many wonderful things, but if we don't take care of our physical and mental wellbeing, we won't get very far.

I think of Elijah, who the Bible tells us was able to walk forty days to his next assignment — after he rested. Sometimes when we're so tired, we lose focus on who God is and what He's done, and is doing in our lives.

Ordinarily I love rainbows because they remind me that God keeps His promises. On the days before I rested, I saw a partial rainbow. When I saw them, I was too exhausted to appreciate their significance. After I'd gotten rest, I was reminded of the beauty of rainbows and the fact I'd never seen rainbows like that two days in a row!

Are you losing sight of the fact that you have so much about which to be joyful in your life? Maybe it's time for you to press the reset button, too!

> Dear Heavenly Father, thank you for rest. Thank you for instituting a day of rest in the beginning when you created the world. Father, help us to make good use of time while realizing we don't need strength to accomplish everything if we keep our trust in You.

> *Come to me, all you who are weary and burdened, and I will give you rest.*
>
> MATTHEW 11:28 NIV

Thought to ponder

Do you find it difficult to take time to rest completely? Why do you think that is?

DAY 17

Childlike Faith

One evening after a frustrating day filled with lots of emotions, as my daughter and I rode in the car a song came on the Christian radio station, K-Love Radio, that seemed to address each question I'd recently faced. As I listened, I kept mumbling, 'hmmm, hmmmm, hmmmm,' answering in the affirmative to the questions being asked.

My daughter, wise beyond her years, asked the exact question on my mind. I wasn't ready to be called out by a seven-year-old in such a manner, so instead I started asking questions.

ME: Do you still believe God for this thing?

HER: Yes.

ME: But you've been asking for this thing for about four years and you still don't have an answer. Do you still believe that God will do it?

HER: Yes.

I was becoming humbled and asked, 'Why do you believe it? Do you believe God has promised it?'

HER: Yes, I believe it because I believe He will do it.

And just like that, I was reminded that the Bible says we must have child-like faith. My daughter fully believes that when she asks God for something, He will do just what she's asking.

I believe He will answer, too — according to His perfect will.

Dear Heavenly Father, I'm so very grateful that You sometimes use others to help teach us lessons, even children. Please help me to exercise child-like faith and to believe that You will provide for my needs according to Your riches in glory.

2 He called a little child to him, and placed the child among them. 3 And he said: "Truly I tell you, unless you change and become like little children, you will never enter the kingdom of heaven. 4 Therefore, whoever takes the lowly position of this child is the greatest in the kingdom of heaven."

Matthew 18:2-4 NIV

Thought to ponder

Is there something for which you've been asking God? How can you change your perspective and exhibit child-like faith?

DAY 18

Promises Kept

I love Fridays!

Friday is typically the day I have no plans when I pick up my daughter, which means we get more one-on-one-time.

On one particular Friday, we'd pre-discussed getting food from McDonald's as her treat for dinner. Because I was already close to the restaurant, I stopped and picked up what I knew she'd want. I even placed it in her car seat so it would be the first thing she saw when she got in the car.

When I picked her up, she reminded me of my promise to treat her to McDonald's. I told her "we'll see," and she started whining and crying and reminding me of my promise. I reiterated "we'll see," and even though she knows I keep my promises to her, her desire for McDonald's food caused her to doubt my ability to keep such a simple promise.

Needless to say, when we went got to the car a few minutes later, her McDonald's Happy Meal was right where I'd left it. I saw her face light up as she expressed surprise that I'd remembered to get it for her.

Isn't this how we treat God?

We ask Him for something and because He doesn't answer right away, we start doubting whether He remembers or will keep His promises. I'm trying to whine and complain a little less as I wait for His promises to come to pass.

Dear Heavenly Father, thank you for the examples that You give us. Thank you for not lying or going back on Your word the way man does. Thank you for keeping Your promises. Thank you for being a good father, whether Your answer is, "No, not yet or yes." Whether or not You answer our prayers the way we want, the fact remains You are a good God and Father.

So is my word that goes out from my mouth: It will not return to me empty, but will accomplish what I desire and achieve the purpose for which I sent it.

Isaiah 55:11 NIV

Thought to ponder

Do you believe that God will do what He has promised to do in your life?

____

____

____

____

____

____

____

____

____

____

DAY 19

Divine Appointments

Have you ever made plans only to have them changed into something better than you could have imagined in your wildest dreams?

A day after my daughter turned five, she asked to go to Elmo's World, known to the rest of us as Sesame Place, for her sixth birthday. In case you haven't picked up on it by now, my daughter got her planning gene from me. The truth is, we both can plan for things years in advance.

Throughout the course of the year, she reminded me that for her sixth birthday she wanted a trip to Elmo's World. So, when we were a few months out, I started planning the logistics. I bought tickets for a set date and then began figuring out how to get there as I don't like long drives.

A few weeks before my daughter's big day, I noticed online that tickets were now cheaper than what I'd pay for them. There was also another reason I needed to change them. I called the box office, even though I knew I'd purchased non-refundable tickets. I laughed and talked with the young woman who'd answered, and despite the non-refundable clause on my tickets, she gave me the better price.

On the day of the party, I took an Uber for the first time. I don't like new adventures, so I planned for several days in advance how to take my first Uber. It was a fifteen-minute drive from the train stop in New Jersey to Sesame Place. The Uber driver was friendly and open, sharing things that I usually never share with strangers. But as I listened to her discuss her life, I opened up and shared some very personal experiences and lessons I'd learned the hard way. When I was about to leave the car, I asked if I could pray for her. By the time I was finished, we were both in tears.

Upon walking in Sesame Place, I knew I'd just had a divine appointment, one only God could have arranged.

Sometimes our divine appointments are for others to help us. Sometimes they're for us to help others. Let us not miss those blessings because we're too self-focused or angry because things didn't work out as we'd originally planned.

Dear Heavenly Father, thank you for showing up for us. Thank you for allowing us to share with strangers during our journeys. Lord, help us to remember that You can make our paths straight, no matter how crooked we may think they are.

Commit to the LORD whatever you do, and he will establish your plans.

PROVERBS 16:3 NIV

Thought to ponder

Have you ever had an encounter that you're convinced was arranged by the Holy Spirit?

DAY 20

Questioning God?

Did you know that it's ok to ask God questions?

One of the most beautiful things I've discovered along my faith journey is that God welcomes my questions. He's even patient with me when I ask the same question over and over because I genuinely don't understand a situation or seek guidance. I believe He loves when I come to Him in humble submission and ask Him to reveal his plan.

My human mind cannot fathom how our awesome God works. There are things I see that make no sense to me, and that is when I question God. God, I don't understand. God, I don't understand why this loved one had to die. God, I don't understand why you're putting me through this situation. Lord, how long?

Imagine if you were in a relationship with someone and you couldn't ask your partner questions? How would that make you feel? Would that endear you to the person or make you want to stay away? God wants us to come to Him with our concerns, no matter how big or small we may think they are.

Before you think I'm making this up, let me share some evidence from the Bible:

Then you will call on Me and come and pray to Me, and I will listen to you. You will seek Me and find Me when you seek Me with all your heart.

JEREMIAH 29:12-13 NIV

Call to me and I will answer you and tell you great and unsearchable things you do not know.

JEREMIAH 33:3 NIV

Then I said, "For how long, Lord?" And he answered: "Until the cities lie ruined and without inhabitant, until the houses are left deserted and the fields ruined and ravaged."

ISAIAH 6:11 NIV

How long, LORD, must I call for help, but you do not listen? Or cry out to you, "Violence!" but you do not save?

HABAKKUK 1:2 NIV

These are only four examples. The first two are a direct promise of what will happen when we call upon or ask God questions. The next two are instances in which God's people asked questions and He answered.

I honestly believe that God delights in answering our questions. But the one thing I've learned is if you ask God questions, He may not answer the way you expect. I've also discovered that to hear what He has to share with you, you have to open your Bible. Many times, we ask questions but don't seek God in His word so we can't understand the instructions He has for us.

I love the book of Job. Job asked God many questions, but when God answered I don't believe Job was prepared for any of His responses. And there are chapters and chapters of God's responses. Do you know what Job's humble response was after hearing all of God's responses?

It's recorded in Job 42:1-6, but I'll highlight verse 5:

My ears had heard of you but now my eyes have seen you.

Dear Heavenly Father, thank you for letting us know it's okay to seek You and ask You questions. Isaiah tells us that your thoughts and ways are higher than our thoughts and ways. Father, there are times we just don't understand how it all fits together. Help us to come to You with our questions, but also help us to understand that You are working things out in ways that we may never understand this side of heaven.

Call to me and I will answer you and tell you great and unsearchable things you do not know.
JEREMIAH 33:3 NIV

Thought to ponder

Are you comfortable asking God questions about what you don't understand? Why or why not?

DAY 21

The Desires Of Our Hearts

When I was first married, my husband and I decided we wanted to get fit together, so we'd either walk or bicycle to the next town over from us and loop back to our neighborhood.

It was on one of those walks that I passed by a schoolyard with a beautiful, well-maintained playground. While it was only one town over from our neighborhood, it seemed as though the two areas were worlds apart. The schools where I lived were rated four on a scale of one to ten. The school we were passing was easily an eight or a nine. I instinctively started thinking, I wish my future kids could go to this better school. But alas, if you didn't live in that town, your kids couldn't attend that school.

Fast forward to when I was divorced and actually had a child nearing school age. I was still living in the neighborhood with the school ranked four on a 10-point scale. Because of the planner in me, I started planning which school she would attend about two years before she was to start kindergarten. Within a matter of months, God opened some doors — I'm still wondering how — and though I was in no position to move, He told me to start looking.

I moved into a house that had sat on the market for a year, as if it was just waiting for me to step out on faith. God had a plan for me. I just had to learn to follow Him even when it didn't make sense financially.

I told my daughter the story of how I wished she could have gone to that school whenever I passed it. But as she called the name out every single time, I realize the only issue I had with it was it's in a very public area allowing everyone to see the kids playing on the playground.

God moved me into that neighborhood, but because of our address, my daughter attended a school that's tucked away. Without me realizing it at the time, God gave me the desires of my heart in even better ways than I'd imagined. I love our home, my daughter's school, and school family.

Heavenly Father, You promised that when we delight in You, You will give us the desires of our hearts. Father, help us to delight in You, but also to trust Your promises. Lord, I know that had I not moved upon your instructions, even though they made no sense to my feeble mind, I would not be where I am today. So Lord, I also ask that You grant us an obedient spirit when You tell us to do something — even if it makes no sense.

Delight yourself in the LORD, and he will give you the desires of your heart.

PSALM 37:4 NIV

Thought to ponder

What is something you can thank God for that He provided in a way much better than you even thought of asking?

DAY 22

Partial Truth

My radio station announced that it could be accessed on Alexa, which was a big surprise to me. Now I'm not a techie, so I wouldn't have thought to ask Alexa to play my radio station, although I know she plays my music from Pandora., Nevertheless, I was excited to try. Of course, my daughter started teasing me, saying if I could really play my station on Alexa, I could stop wearing out Pandora.

The next morning, I asked Alexa to play the station according to the instructions I'd heard on the radio. After hearing my request, Alexa announced, playing K-Love on radio.com, ninety-eight point seven. Hmmm. Wasn't my radio station ninety-six point seven? Oh well, I thought, she said the same name so it's probably ok. When the songs started playing, I didn't recognize the first song but didn't think much of it. I didn't recognize the second one either, and soon realized this was much more of a rock station.

I decided to give Alexa clearer instructions: "Alexa, play K-Love Radio on ninety-six point seven." Sure enough, this time Alexa played the right radio station.

I later remembered a devotion I'd read earlier in the week on the Devotable app. The author told her class that 'there is no god' is in the Bible. Her students were shocked, but she asked them to find it in the Bible. Psalm 14:1 says "The fool says in his heart, 'There is no God.' They are corrupt, their deeds are vile; there is no one who does good."

I started thinking... How many times do we have partial information and we take it as truth, or as 'gospel' as the old folks say? This is why it's so important to know what we believe for ourselves. We need to study the Bible for ourselves to ensure we don't rely solely on what we're being told.

Had I not known what I was looking for, I could easily have been misled by Alexa. Had the kids not gone searching for themselves, they might have believed the excerpt of the verse that was shared, not realizing it was taken out of context.

Dear Heavenly Father, thank you for Your unfailing wisdom. Help us to be discerning in what we hear. Help us to do our own studying of the Bible so we may show ourselves approved by You.

Study to shew thyself approved unto God, a workman that needeth not to be ashamed, rightly dividing the word of truth.

2 Timothy 2:15 KJV

Thought to ponder

Are you ever tempted to simply take what you hear as the absolute truth? How can you do your own due diligence to confirm what's being said?

DAY 23

Holding Hands

I just love walking down the street holding my daughter's hand. Thankfully, she still enjoys holding mine as well.

There have been many times when we've been walking together, holding hands, , and I've felt her stumble but gripped her hand tightly enough to prevent her from falling. Sometimes she gets shaken up by the near fall, but I remind her that's one of the reasons we hold hands - so I can protect her.

Whenever that has happened, I've had the same thought: That's how it is when we hold onto God's unchanging hands. We might stumble, but we will not fall.

I just came across the verse that supports my thought: Psalm 37:24 NIV: "Though he may stumble, he will not fall, for the Lord upholds him with His hand."

Are you feeling like you're repeatedly stumbling? Are you holding onto the unchanging hands of our Lord? Remember, He promises that we will not fall if we keep holding onto Him. Just like my daughter keeps holding onto my hand and it keeps her from falling, we need to hold onto His unchanging hand as well.

Heavenly Father, thank you for not letting go of our hands. Help us to realize that it's never you who lets go; it's us. Lord, if we have let go of You for any reason, help us to come back to you as soon as possible, knowing that we are secure with You and, though we may stumble, we will not fall, as your word promises.

Though he may stumble, he will not fall, for the Lord upholds him with his hand.

PSALM 37:24 NIV

Thought to ponder

What can you do in your life to keep from stumbling?

____

____

____

____

____

____

____

____

____

____

____

What can you do in your life to keep from stumbling?

____

DAY 24

Spending Uninterrupted Time

A few days ago, I was struggling. I wasn't sure why, but something just felt completely off. When that happens, I usually start analyzing what's different in my routine.

As I was evaluating what changes I'd made, I knew the culprit was how I was spending my quiet time. I was still awakening early to have quiet time before everyone else got up, but it was more distracted quiet time than focused quiet time.

There were Facebook and Instagram messages to be checked.

Text messages were coming in as I was reading.

Emails were calling my name.

I was very distracted during my quiet time.

Then I received a few messages from my friend this week.

1. Do something nice for yourself today.

2. You can't pour from an empty cup. Make sure you nourish your spirit first. Have a blessed day!! (I'd told two special ladies this just earlier in the day, not realizing I needed to take my own medicine.)

3. Activities without purpose are a drain on your life. Be intentional about what you choose to do today.

Three different messages on three different days, each of which spoke directly to my heart. I knew I needed to be more intentional about how I spent my quiet time.

Is this something you, too, need to do? Let's do it together.

Dear Heavenly Father, may spending quiet time with You never become just a routine or something for us to check off of a list once it's completed. Help us to be intentional and focused about the time we spend in Your presence. Thank you for friends who speak to our hearts and make a difference without even knowing they're doing so.

But whose delight is in the law of the LORD, and who meditates on his law day and night.

PSALM 1:2 NIV

Thought to ponder

Do you need to be more intentional about how you spend your quiet time?

DAY 25

You Are LOVED!

Do you know that God loves you? Like, really really loves you? Do you know He thinks highly of you?

Today I want to share a few verses with you, just to remind you (and me) that the God of the universe loves us with an everlasting love, one that's not comparable to anything you'll ever feel on earth.

So God created man in his own image, in the image of God he created him; male and female he created them.

GENESIS 1:27 NIV

Before I formed you in the womb I knew you, before you were born I set you apart; I appointed you as a prophet to the nations.

JEREMIAH 1:5 NIV

For you created my inmost being; you knit me together in my mother's womb. 14 I praise You because I am fearfully and wonderfully made; Your works are wonderful, I know that full well.

PSALM 139:13-14 NIV

And even the very hairs of your head are all numbered.

MATTHEW 10:30 NIV

You have made them a little lower than the angels and crowned them with glory and honor.

PSALM 8:5 NIV

*See what great love the Father has lavished on us, that
we should be called children of God! And that is what
we are! The reason the world does not know us is that
it did not know him. 2 Dear friends, now we are children
of God, and what we will be has not yet been made
known. But we know that when Christ appears, we shall
be like him, for we shall see him as he is.*

1 JOHN 3:1-2 NIV

No matter what emotions you may be feeling today, or how you think others feel about you, I want to remind you that you are loved.

Dear Heavenly Father, thank you for taking such care to make us, even from the beginning of time. Your word said everything was created, except men and women, because You took the time to form us and saw our needs from the beginning of time. Then You pronounced us "very good." Father, help us to always remember just how you think of us, and remind us that is all that matters.

And even the very hairs of your head are all numbered.

MATTHEW 10:30 NIV

Thought to ponder

Do you believe that you are truly loved by God? What are some of the ways you see evidence of His love?

DAY 26
In The Fullness Of Time

My friend and I were having a conversation about the things that are happening in my life. She's a new friend, so she's seeing what's happening from a very current perspective. I've shared a little about my writing experiences and how I got started a few years ago with no intention of sharing what I wrote with anyone. That was my intention. God had a different plan.

As I'm thinking about it, I was living out Proverbs 16:9 ESV, which says "The heart of man plans his way, but the LORD establishes his steps."

I went from writing just for me to publishing a whole devotional book.

That may surprise you. To be honest, it surprises me too. I will still tell you that I'm not a writer, yet God has seen fit to use me. I did not know what I was doing when I started writing a devotional book, and there are many days that I still wonder about it all. Yet God has still seen fit to use me. I continued writing when I had no idea where it was all going. Yet God still saw fit to use me.

Sometimes we're waiting on God to deliver something to us or to answer a prayer. But sometimes in those times of waiting, we forget that there's a right time and a wrong time.

In Galatians 4:4 ESV it says, "But when the fullness of time had come, God sent forth his Son, born of woman, born under the law."

The right time for Jesus to be born had come. Not before and not after.

Dear Heavenly Father, Lord, we are waiting for You. We are waiting for things that You have promised us. Father, help us to remember that You do all things well, and You do things "in the fullness of time". Help us not to get weary of doing what You have called us to do, but instead to realize that in the right time, You will fulfill your promises to us.

I am the LORD; in its time I will do this swiftly.

Isaiah 60:22b NIV

Thought to ponder

Are you waiting for God to move in your life? Do you believe it is the right time? Do you think God thinks it's the right time?

DAY 27

Would You Have Stopped?

I try to be very candid with the lessons I'm learning and what I share. To be honest, this one is a hard one, but I'll share it anyway.

My mommy friend with whom I take the train texted me midafternoon to confirm what train I'd be on. I shared the train time, which was twenty minutes earlier than our usual time and meant we'd be riding a train that doesn't make all of the local stops. We agreed to meet at our usual spot.

When the appointed time came, my friend instead called to ask me to pick up her daughter from school. She thought she wasn't going to be able to pick her up on time due to an unfolding emergency. Her niece had called, she explained, because she had seen a little boy with an older lady who was in distress.

When my friend arrived on scene, an ambulance had already been called, but hadn't yet arrived. Because the older lady was unconscious, my friend was concerned about the little boy. He was unkempt and appeared as if he hadn't been bathed in weeks. Her first thought was to go into the store to buy him clean underwear and something to wear, which she accomplished before the ambulance arrived. Ultimately, she still caught the train we'd agreed to take.

After we met up and she was telling me what happened, I started wondering whether I would have done what she had done. And I honestly don't know the answer. I'm always running, and if I left the office so I could catch my train, I really can't say whether I would have allowed my schedule to go off track. I just don't know.

I pray that the next time something like that happens, if I witness it, I will exercise enough compassion to pause and tend to those in need.

Heavenly Father, may I never be too busy to see the needs of those around me.

For I was hungry and you gave me something to eat, I was thirsty and you gave me something to drink, I was a stranger and you invited me in, I needed clothes and you clothed me, I was sick and you looked after me, I was in prison and you came to visit me.

MATTHEW 25:35-36 NIV

Thought to ponder

Would you have stopped? How can you show hospitality and compassion to those in need around you?

DAY 28

Are You Preparing?

I've been asking God for something for a few years. Like, seriously, a few years. I believe God is in the process of answering my request.

One day, while thinking about my request and the progression of my life to that point, I realized I wasn't prepared were God to answer my request that day.

It became glaringly obvious to me that while I was asking, I wasn't prepared to receive such a gift.

Imagine that! Asking for something, fully expecting to receive it, anticipating it and all the while not being in a position to receive it when it comes.

As a result, I came to realize that while I may be asking for something, God needs to know I'm ready to receive what He has for me.

Are you asking God to enlarge your territory? If you received that gift today, would you be ready to manage the resources that God has sent your way?

Are you asking God for a new home? If you received that gift today, would you be able to take care of the expenses and other responsibilities that come with owning a home?

Many of us ask for gifts, including me, but don't adequately prepare for their arrival. This is part of faith and obedience — doing the next thing even when we don't have our answers yet.

Dear Heavenly Father, thank you for such poignant reminders that along with asking and waiting, we must be prepared. Even when we don't know what to do, please help us to do the next small thing in an act of faith that you will hear and answer our prayers.

Prepare yourself and be ready, you and all your companies that are gathered about you; and be a guard for them.

Ezekiel 38:7 NKJV

Thought to ponder

What are you asking God to do in your life? Are you ready and prepared to receive His gift?

DAY 29

A Changing Season

I love mangoes!

Wait. Did I mention that I absolutely love mangoes?

A few years ago, I was in Jamaica in June, at the peak of mango season. The fruit was plentiful. Every tree was laden with ripe mangoes. And mangoes had fallen under the trees everywhere I went.

Due to family reasons, I had to go back a month later. I was excited at the prospect of once again seeing trees laden with mangoes and being able to eat the fruit as snacks before breakfast, before lunch and after dinner.

As soon as I was driving home from the airport, I realized the difference. There were far less mangoes on the trees, especially ripe ones. Even so, I was able to purchase and enjoy some, but it got me thinking...

Sometimes we're in bountiful seasons with no end in sight.

Conversely, sometimes we're in seasons without everything we want with no end in sight.

Had I gone a month or two later, I'm sure there would have been even fewer mangoes, if any at all. Mango season in Jamaica is around the same time every year, and they become scarce after that.

Are you in a season in which you feel like you don't have all you need or want? I want to reassure you that if you just hold on a little bit longer, your season will change. We're reminded in the Bible that everything has a season.

I pray your season of bounty comes soon.

Dear Heavenly Father, thank you for allowing seasons to come and go. We would not appreciate the season of bounty if we had it all of the time, and we might not be reminded that we need to rely on You for our provisions. And Lord, if we are in a season of bounty right now, we thank You and ask that You provide for those who are without.

For everything there is a season, a time for every activity under heaven. 2 A time to plant and a time to harvest.
ECCLESIASTES 3:1, 2B NLT

Thought to ponder

Which season are you walking through right now? Is it one of bounty or seemingly scarcity?

DAY 30

Give Thanks

A few summers ago, I thanked God because someone was mean to me.

Before you start wondering if I've lost it, let me explain.

I'm an early riser, and I love to go to the beach. I went to the beach on my early morning excursion, expecting to pay my usual ten dollars for the parking fee. When I got there, the attendant asked for ID. Parking for town residents is ten dollars, twenty-five for non-residents. I had been going to this beach for the last three summers since I became a resident. I produced my ID that had my old address on the front and my new address written on the back, acceptable as long as you've updated it with the state.

I handed him a twenty-dollar bill and waited for my change. The attendant, upon seeing my old address, said that was my address. I explained to him that I'd moved years ago and my new address was on the back. I also explained to him that I'd been coming to that same beach for the last three years, using that ID without an issue. He proceeded to lecture me on how I'd been getting away with that and said he wasn't going to charge me the full twenty-five-dollar non-resident fee but was going to charge me twenty dollars. He had the gall to say it as though he was doing me a favor, giving me a deal. Well, needless to say that was not a deal to me. I kindly asked for my twenty-dollar bill and told him I would leave.

The irony of this situation is that a few days prior, I'd gone to the Department of Motor Vehicles to update my soon-to-be-expired license. Officials provided me with the temporary paper pass, which

I inadvertently left when I changed my purse. They were in the process of mailing the permanent one.

I was annoyed. All I was looking to do was enjoy some quiet moments at the beach.

I made a U-turn out of the lot and left. As I was driving, I decided to find another entrance where I wouldn't pay for parking, but likely pay for beach entrance. I was ok with that as it was still cheaper than twenty dollars.

As I drove down to another entrance, in another beach town, I easily found parking. The employees were already at the gate as it was about eight fifty-seven and they started collecting entrance fees at nine. I walked right by them, sat on the beach for a few hours and enjoyed my much-needed quiet time. After a few hours, I walked right by those same employees without having to exchange any money.

Do you understand why I was thankful the attendant was mean to me?

I can laugh about this situation now. Initially I was annoyed at the parking attendant for being unreasonable and for trying to beat me out of ten dollars, but in the end his attitude turned out to be a blessing that saved me ten dollars that morning.

Sometimes when we're facing annoying situations and can't see how things will work out, we need to remember Paul, who reminds us to give thanks in all things.

Trust me, I know how difficult those instructions are. But when we start giving thanks and praising God no matter what, it changes our perspective and takes the focus from us and puts it onto God.

Dear Heavenly Father, I've used a simple example to demonstrate that sometimes we have to let go of our attitudes and let loose our praise and thanksgiving to You. But Lord, I don't take it lightly when we are truly going through difficult situations. Your word says to give thanks in all things. Help us to change our attitudes and our demeanor so that we may be able to say that though we are going through hard times, we will still be able to say that You are good and give You thanks.

In everything give thanks; for this is the will of God in Christ Jesus for you.

1 THESSALONIANS 5:18 NKJV

Thought to ponder

What is something that at first was an annoyance but turned out to be a blessing for you?

DAY 31
Our Expectations

Around July each year, since my daughter was born, I'm filled with an overwhelming sense of gratitude. She's turning six shortly, but I've learned so much from her in my daily interactions.

This is one such lesson.

She planned a year ago to go to Sesame Place for her birthday. I think she received the so-called "planning ahead" trait from me. So, a few days after turning five, she asked if we could go to Elmo's World, otherwise known as Sesame Place.

I promised that we could go, and she wouldn't let me forget it, even if I tried.

Thunderstorms were predicted for pretty much the whole week. I love including her in decision making because I believe this is how she will learn to make wise decisions. So, I gave her the option of still going on her actual birthday, though the forecast was rainy and overcast, or on Friday, the subsequent day, when it was supposed to be clearer and sunny.

She was adamant she didn't want to go on Friday because her class would be making fruit smoothies and she didn't want to miss out on the fun.

I tried to convince her that the weather would be much nicer on Friday. Then I asked her, "What happens at Elmo's World?" Her response was "you get to see characters walking around".

Sesame Place is so much more than that. It's a park with rides and a water park that's geared specifically towards smaller kids.

Even after my explanation, she still didn't want to forego Friday smoothies.

Try as I might, I couldn't understand her logic.

Then I got a gentle reminder that I operate like that quite frequently. I'm willing to bypass things that have a longer-term effect for quick results. Her smoothie-making class would probably last a half hour. Her trip to Sesame place had been in the works for a whole year and would last a full day.

Are you tempted to give in to near-term satisfaction because you can't see the longer-term view? You can't seem to see how much planning has been done behind the scenes for you, and you can't see what lies ahead?

Dear Heavenly Father, help us to have the perspective that You have. Help us to see things the way You do. Help us to not make hasty decisions based on just the short term, but to factor in the longer-term effects.

Commit to the LORD whatever you do, and he will establish your plans.

PROVERBS 16:3 NIV

Thought to ponder

How can you commit your plans to the Lord in a better way than you do now?

DAY 32

Our Disappointments

I think I've gotten into a rhythm of posting a blog thought once a week, mainly on the weekend.

As Friday approached, I realized I hadn't seen any lessons that would translate into a thought, so I started praying for something. Saturday came. Nothing. Sunday came. Nothing. Sunday evening came. Still nothing.

I had almost given up on sharing, but I believe I have a commitment with God to share once per week. I mentioned it to my author friend and she suggested I repost a previous blog. That would work too. Except there was no revelation of a previously discussed topic that came to mind.

In a quick moment, I decided to ask that same friend to guest blog for me, and she quickly agreed. I asked her to send me the post, and she did without hesitation.

When I shared it, one of the responses I received was from a woman who said it was an answer to her prayer request from earlier that day.

Then I thought back to the day before, when one of the young ladies I watched grow up, publicly shared her testimony about being locked out of her apartment. The answer to her prayer? Her sister's flight was delayed, enabling her to go to the airport to get the key without having to pay for a locksmith. This young lady challenged us to try to look at our situations differently.

I also thought about the fact that sometimes our disappointments can be someone's blessing. One friend's flight was delayed – to her disappoint, but was enough time to allow the prayer to be answered for her sister to be able to get a key to get into her apartment.

Can we see that sometimes God uses a situation that's disappointing to us to answer someone else's prayer?

I've had this thought, too: I want answers to my prayers, but I realize sometimes there are others with prayer requests and God may be using my seemingly setbacks and disappointments to answer someone else's prayer.

Dear Heavenly Father, help us to see with spiritual eyes. Please change our perspective and remind us that we cannot have a 'Me only" attitude when we pray. Help us to let go of the reigns of our lives so that You can reign supremely.

8 *For my thoughts are not your thoughts, neither are your ways my ways," declares the LORD.* **9** *"As the heavens are higher than the earth, so are my ways higher than your ways and my thoughts than your thoughts."*

ISAIAH 55:8-9 NIV

Thought to ponder

How do you react when you don't receive the answers you expect from God, or the way you expect them?

DAY 33

Distractions

People across the world are "staying home" due to the corona-virus, also known as COVID-19. My daughter and I have been home together for the last 17 days or so. I'm trying to work from home and also be "teacher" as I help her with the assignments from her real teacher.

As it's been a season of unexpected change for all of us, my daughter and I are trying to manage as best as we can. I'm also trying to give grace – as we are all navigating this new sense of loss – of so many things. For me, the loss of social interaction has been difficult. I'm sure she's feeling a sense of loss as well, but may not be able to articulate it as well as I can. I still try to keep her on a routine. It's not perfect, but it gives us both a sense of structure and normalcy in what we are each facing. Part of that routine is spending the earlier parts of the morning doing school work.

Her escape has been watching YouTube. Because it gives me time to focus on my work, I've allowed it. That and I recognize that we each take our mental breaks differently. On this particular morn-ing, I was asking her to do some schoolwork and she found a way to complain about every bit of it. I'd spent quality time with God that morning and managed to remain calm during all the whining and hysterics; however, I took her tablet from her, telling her that until she focused on what she needed to do she wasn't getting it back.

She went back to her assignment, but was still crying and playing with her fake boot (don't ask... long story). As I told her that if she didn't resume working and stop playing with her boot, I was going to take away anything that distracted her. I felt my heart instantly convicted and had to say out loud, "Lord have mercy."

My heart had indeed been convicted. God is a jealous God and doesn't want anything competing for our attention. I know He's telling me that He'll remove anything from my life that is distracting my thoughts from Him.

I wonder if this is what this difficult season is about? I know I've been learning some lessons in Jeremiah 16, and as I've seen how it applies to what we're experiencing in today's world, I know there's a portion that talks about God not being willing to share our attention with any other gods.

I pray I am learning this lesson.

> Dear Heavenly Father, these are extremely difficult days, but I'm not telling you anything you don't already know. Father, if there are any idols in our lives, whether intentional or unintentional, I ask that you show us and remove them.

> **10** *"When you tell these people all this and they ask you, 'Why has the LORD decreed such a great disaster against us? What wrong have we done? What sin have we committed against the LORD our God?'*
> **11** *then say to them, 'It is because your ancestors forsook me,' declares the LORD, 'and followed other gods and served and worshiped them. They forsook me and did not keep my law."*
>
> JEREMIAH 16: 10-11 NIV

Thought to ponder

As you read these words, is there something or someone that comes to mind that you have been putting ahead of God?

DAY 34

I See No Train Traffic

"I see no train traffic" were the words my daughter uttered as she waited not-so-patiently for the train to move.

She has always loved riding the train, and on this day, I had the pleasure of taking her into the city with me on my early morning commute. The train had stopped, dropped off and picked up its new passengers and closed the doors, but was still waiting in the station, not moving.

The announcer came on the intercom to say we had to wait on train traffic to clear before proceeding. My daughter looked up from the comfort of my lap and commented, "I see no train traffic" and just as quickly put her head down back in her comfortable spot.

I chuckled and commented that we were sitting about four cars in with a lot of things blocking our view and the driver had a clear view of what was ahead.

Somehow this turned into a sobering moment for me.

How often do I tell God that it's time to move on my request? I somehow forget that He's the one driving, and He has a clear view of what's in front and what lies ahead. He can see from the beginning to the end and everywhere in between. But from my limited view, I can see only what's directly in front of me, and sometimes what I'm seeing isn't even the whole picture.

Dear Heavenly Father, thank you for perspective. Thank you for seeing what lies ahead of us. Help us to trust that You know and see all, especially when our limited view is telling us that something doesn't make sense, knowing that during those times you've already worked out the details.

The path of the righteous is level; you, the Upright One, make the way of the righteous smooth.

Isaiah 26:7 NIV

Thought to ponder

Do you trust that God sees all that is before you, with no obstructions?

DAY 35

God Can Handle Our Honesty

I was in a crappy mood one Friday.

I'm not quite sure how to fully explain why, but I was in a funk. I realized I was snippy with my colleagues, and even someone I didn't work closely with teased and said my energy was amiss. I laughed it off, but knew he'd hit the nail on the head.

I understand that life and seasons change, but sometimes those changes and seasons are hard to handle. And on that particular day, I wasn't handling things well.

The cloud cover stayed with me throughout the day and well into the evening.

As I was walking out of the office to head home, I started talking to God. There was something specific that I'd wanted that day and hadn't gotten. As I walked, I poured my heart out to God, telling Him exactly how I was feeling and why. I've learned that God can handle my honest emotions, even when I'm having a difficult time even articulating my feelings.

No sooner than I got home, I received call. I knew exactly why, but at the moment I wasn't ready for the honest conversation that was needed. So, I ended the call, explaining that I wasn't in the best of moods.

I still needed to work out with God how to deal with what I was feeling and ask for guidance on how to proceed. I now realize that God cares about even the small details of our lives. He provided the guidance I needed, enabling me to move forward.

Is there something that you have been reluctant to tell God? Rest assured; nothing catches God off guard. He can handle your funky moods, your bad energy and what you think you can't share with anyone else.

Dear Heavenly Father, thank you for knowing us and our personalities even before we were formed in our mother's wombs — and for loving us all the same. Help us to realize that You can handle our honest emotions and You welcome us with open arms when we want to share with you.

26 *In the same way, the Spirit helps us in our weakness. We do not know what we ought to pray for, but the Spirit himself intercedes for us through wordless groans.* **27** *And he who searches our hearts knows the mind of the Spirit, because the Spirit intercedes for God's people in accordance with the will of God.*

ROMANS 8:26-27 NIV

Thought to ponder

What discussion have you been reluctant to have with God? I promise you; He already knows.

DAY 36

Directions

I work in one of the busiest cities in the world. On my way to work the other day, as I was walking on the sidewalk, I gazed up at one of the tallest buildings lining the sky. I'm a true to the core New Yorker and know that there's no stopping to gaze at anything — only continued movement while gazing.

As I glanced up while walking, I started veering to the right. I quickly adjusted my vision to directly in front of me; however, because I wanted to confirm what I suspected just happened to me, I looked up again. This time I started veering to the left. Again, I had to refocus my vision and look straight ahead.

In that moment, I remembered my driving instructor telling me years ago that as I was driving I needed to look where I wanted to go. Wherever I focused my attention, the instructor said, would likely be where my car would go.

I think it's the same in our Christian walk. We need to keep our eyes on where we want to go. If we get distracted and start looking at the things around us, we will lose focus on what our main goal is and should be — pleasing God and experiencing eternal life. A thought comes to mind: this is the way you should go, neither veer to the left nor to the right. The only way we will do this is by keeping our attention completely focused on where we are going.

Proverbs 3:5-6 states, "Trust in the LORD with all thine heart; and lean not unto thine own understanding. In all thy ways acknowledge Him, and He shall direct thy paths."

I pray that you will join me in asking for constant direction so that we will know when we are veering to the right or to the left.

Dear Heavenly Father, thank you for guiding us. Please show us the way we should go. Help us to keep our focus on You so that we won't get distracted and bogged down by the cares of this world. Instead, help us learn how to completely rely on You to get us to our destinations safely.

You will keep him in perfect peace, Whose mind is stayed on You, Because he trusts in You.

Isaiah 26:3 NKJV

Thought to ponder

Where is your focus currently? Is it on the world, on yourself or on God? Do you need to adjust your gaze?

DAY 37

Cast Your Cares

A few weeks ago, I started a load of laundry. Nothing out of the norm. I put the clothes in the washing machine, pushed the settings buttons and continued doing other chores around my home. When it neared time for the spin cycle to run, it sounded like a donkey was in our home, which, of course, terrified my daughter.

The sound was both funny and terrifying, because I didn't know where it was coming from initially. Once I located the source, I turned off the machine, which was full of water and clothes. I gave it a few minutes and restarted it. Same results. It sounded like a braying donkey.

I called my dad who promptly told me to call my plumber. Unfortunately, my dad was unable to make it to me.

I gave it a few days and tried to use the washing machine again. Same results. As soon as it got to a certain point in the wash cycle, the noise started and I had to quickly stop it.

This went on for two weeks: me trying with the same load of laundry, only to get the same results, braying sounds and all.

It finally occurred to me that I could remove the clothes and squeeze out enough water then attempt to dry them. My plumber still hadn't had time to come diagnose the problem. I proceeded with the arduous task of wringing out my clothes but soon grew tired because there were so many pieces.

I called my mom to explain my frustration, and she shared that she'd overloaded her machine and gotten some funky results. The thought had never even occurred to me that my machine had been overloaded. As I'd already removed about half of the clothes, I decided to try running the rinse and spin cycles.

Voilà!!!

Are you overloaded and trying to do too much? Are you feeling the weight of an over-packed calendar or upcoming holiday schedule? Jesus reminds us to cast our cares on Him, because He cares for us.

Today, I won't overload my washer or my life because I realize everything has its limit, especially my capacity to handle what life throws at me. Cast your cares on your Heavenly Father. I promise you; He cares for you.

> Dear Heavenly Father, thank you for this simple reminder that I was not meant to carry such a heavy load. You have promised me that if I choose Your yoke, it won't be too heavy for me to bear. Help me to choose You. Help me to recognize when I have overloaded my life and am running beyond capacity. Help me to understand that, just like my washing machine, my life will display signs when I am overloaded or overburdened.

Cast all your anxiety on him because he cares for you.

1 PETER 5:7 NIV

Thought to ponder

Are you feeling overwhelmed? What can you do to lighten the load you're carrying?

DAY 38
Shortcut

Some time ago, I had a package that I needed to send via UPS. I'm a very last-minute person. I typically get the job done, but usually very close to the deadline. True to my nature, I'd created the package and probably had it next to me for much of the day. As I was leaving at the end of the workday, with a very tight timeframe to catch my train, I remembered that the package still needed to be dropped off at UPS. In my haste, I asked someone who was new to the team to take it and drop it off for me. Great! Done, right?

NOT!

As I was sitting on the train, I received a text message from a colleague. She said the package was erroneously dropped off in the regular USPS mailbox. Oy! She said she'd recreate the package as she knew it was time sensitive, but I'd still have to figure out how to retrieve the original package from the regular mailbox.

The next day, I spent about half the day trying to coordinate with security to ensure that when the mailman came, I'd be able to get it back. I even provided my cell numbers to ensure I got the call. The package contained sensitive client information and I couldn't have it falling into the wrong hands.

While I was going through it and getting frustrated by the process, I thought how annoying! If I had just taken the extra three minutes to drop it off myself, I wouldn't have been in this predicament. Instead, those three minutes added extra time to my colleague's workday and cost me to spend nearly half the next day trying to retrieve it.

How many times do we try to take shortcuts with God? Remember that eleven-day trip from Egypt? Forty years later!

Seriously, I hope I remember this lesson the next time I'm tempted to try to take a shortcut.

Dear Heavenly Father, thank you for these lessons. Sometimes it's frustrating as we're going through the process, but please help us to remember these lessons and process them in the right frame of mind to ensure we learn from them in the future.

But do not forget this one thing, dear friends: With the Lord a day is like a thousand years, and a thousand years are like a day.

2 Peter 3:8 NIV

Thought to ponder

Is there an area in your life for which you've tried to take a shortcut? How did it turn out?

DAY 39

Do You Have The Right Tools?

We had tenants who caused extensive damage to our home. Now that they're gone, it's time to clean up and rebuild. It's been a long journey, but we're thankful it's over.

As a part of the major repair process, we ripped up the carpets. Our friend came and helped. There were boards with nails that remained after the major job was done. I looked around and because I was eager to do something, I said I could handle it.

Hmmm. Maybe I should have thought that through.

He left his carpet tool and cautioned that I needed to have the right tool for the job.

The following day when I was doing the hard labor of lifting up the staple nails with the flat part of the tool he'd left, all I kept thinking was how grateful I was to have the right tool. Had I tried with anything other than what had been left, I knew it wouldn't have worked.

This got me thinking...

As a Christian, do I have the right tools and am I using them in my daily life?

I know God has endowed us with different gifts and talents, but to exercise those gifts and talents we must also use the tools the Bible tells us.

I consider the fruit of the spirit some of the tools that will make us good Christians when we actively use them.

The fruit of the Spirit is: love, joy, peace, patience, kindness, goodness, faithfulness, gentleness and self-control.

Although there are nine items, they are viewed as one combined fruit, hence the grammar 'is.'

> Dear Heavenly Father, thank you for your love. Thank you for supplying us with the right tools so we can do the job You've called us to do. Help us to be diligent in our tasks for You.

> **22** *But the fruit of the Spirit is love, joy, peace, forbearance, kindness, goodness, faithfulness,*
> **23** *gentleness and self-control. Against such things there is no law.*
>
> GALATIANS 5:22-23 NIV

Thought to ponder

Are you using the right tools for the job? How can you become better?

DAY 40
Will You Say "Yes"?

I recently presented a workshop at my church's conference-wide training for Treasurers, Clerks and Stewardship.

If someone had told me last year when I attended that I'd be listed in the program as a presenter that at this year's event, I wouldn't have believed it.

But God...

As I look back over some of the things that have happened in the course of the last year or so, I'm amazed and humbled.

As our church was accepting nominations for positions at the end of 2018, my friend and church colleague called to tell me I'd been nominated for a combined role of Finance Chair and Stewardship Director. My initial thought/response was nope, I'm too busy. He shared that he would be on my team and asked me to pray about my decision. I VERY reluctantly told him I would pray, knowing my response was no.

Very shortly after praying, I received the nudge, "you say you want to make a change, but now when given the opportunity you're saying no."

God, do I really have to?

I reluctantly accepted the positions. Within a matter of weeks, I met one of the pastors who answered prayers I didn't even realize I'd had actually prayed, yet God saw fit to answer.

I look back and see how God has worked with my simple "yes," opening doors I couldn't have imagined.

Are you expecting God to open doors for you despite your refusal to do what He's asking of you? Sometimes to get to certain doors, you have to be willing to walk through doors that look like nothing you expected.

Dear Heavenly Father, thank you for the wisdom to say yes, even when I didn't want to. Thank you for stepping in when we show ourselves faithful with the little things and believe the promises that when we are faithful with little, You will provide us much.

6 *"Alas, Sovereign LORD," I said, "I do not know how to speak; I am too young."* **7** *But the LORD said to me, "Do not say, 'I am too young.' You must go to everyone I send you to and say whatever I command you.* **8** *Do not be afraid of them, for I am with you and will rescue you,"* *declares the LORD.*

JEREMIAH 1:6-8 NIV

Thought to ponder

Is there a request that keeps coming up that will take you out of your comfort zone? Are you ready to say "yes?"

DAY 41

Change Your Perspective

This past week was a rough one. It felt like so many unexpected things were happening and as though money was flowing out of my account like water. I could definitely relate to a saying that my friend shared, "in like drops and out like a waterfall," as obligation after obligation kept popping up.

By the end of the week, I just wanted to go home and relax I passed an acquaintance when I got off the train who asked if I was getting ready for the sabbath and I responded "yes, to go home and rest". Within seconds of passing him, I saw a note on my car. . As long as it's not a ticket, I'm fine, I thought. After seeing that it wasn't a ticket, I pulled it off and that's when I noticed my driver's side mirror was completely broken off.

Could this week get any worse?

I followed the directions of the note, telling me to go to the nearby store as they might have a camera to see who had swiped my mirror. They did not have any recording of the incident. Instead, I ended up back to the person who originally wrote it. I thanked her. It was thoughtful and she had even put it in a plastic covering so that it wouldn't be damaged by the rain.

I got home, feeling a bit down trodden and like the week had kicked my butt. After settling down and texting a friend to complain, I got a phone call. Shortly thereafter, another friend showed up at my door with newsletters for my church and some money from book sales. I'm guessing in that moment he had no clue that he was bringing me hope and a reminder that God sees and knows all.

The newsletter contained three articles written by me. The number of articles and money were much more than I would have even thought to ask God for — had I asked.

The cash was a timely reminder that God takes care of all of my needs.

By the next morning, I realized God wanted to change my perspective so He showed me that He'd taken care of the waterfall by filling me with lots of drops from different places.

Is there something for which you, too, need to change your perspective?

> Dear Heavenly Father, thank you for caring about the smallest details and reminding us that You can take care of our every need. Thank you for setting things in motion to show us that You care, even as we go about our normal routines.

> *And my God will meet all your needs according to the riches of his glory in Christ Jesus.*
>
> PHILIPPIANS 4:19 NIV

Thought to ponder

Is there something that you need to change your perspective on too?

DAY 42

Worship While You Wait

Have you ever gone through a situation feeling confident you knew the eventual outcome, only to have it turn out differently?

Yesterday my mom and I had just that experience.

We've been in the court system because of a non-paying tenant for a year now.

The last time we were in court in November, we signed an agreement stipulating the tenant would leave at the end of December, we would ask for no more rent and the tenant couldn't ask for any more time in the property without being subject to all back rent. This was a professional tenant. Unfortunately, they had done this to other landlords. He was in violation of the agreement but had us back in court.

We sat all day waiting to see a judge, assuming all the while that he'd rule in our favor.

He didn't.

He gave them another twenty-one days to continue living for free in our property without having to pay back rent to us.

We had prayed continually over this time. We had fasted. We had asked others to pray for us.

How do we reconcile asking God for something and continuing to hear no, or not yet?

How do you not lose faith while asking and waiting?

As I was preparing to write this, I was provided the answer.

It comes from Jesus in the garden of Gethsemane. He was praying and asking God to take away the pain He was about to suffer. He didn't want to do it, but He said, "Not as I will, but Your will be done." His desire was for His Father's will, not what he wanted.

Sometimes when we're going through experiences, we can't truly focus on what's happening. The enemy tries to attack our minds and convince us that God isn't listening to our cries.

When this happens, what do you do?

You worship while you wait. You take the focus off of what you think you should have done or how someone else should have responded and trust that God knows all and knows best. You ask God to increase your faith a little more each day as you continue to trust Him and wait for the outcome you desire.

In life we are certain to have disappointments, but let us not lose heart. Let us run the race that has been set before us. Let us trust that God is weaving together a tapestry so beautiful that it will be made evident to all in His perfect timing.

> Dear Lord, thank you for experiences that mold us into who You want us to be. Help us to see them for what they are: temporary learning situations that will ultimately come to an end. Help us to learn from these experiences and to give You much-deserved praise and glory even while we're going through them.

> *Now faith is confidence in what we hope for and assurance about what we do not see.*
> HEBREWS 11:1 NIV

Thought to ponder

How can you worship while you are going through a difficult season?

DAY 43
Standing Your Ground

Have you ever gotten in trouble for standing up for something you believe in?

I came across the well-known story of the three Hebrew boys in Daniel III. They refused to bow down to the idol that King Nebuchadnezzar had built.

I read through the whole chapter and got chills by the way they responded.

Let me give you a little background...

These boys, Shadrach, Meshach and Abednego were taken captive from their homeland, their names changed to reflect Babylonian culture. Even though their names changed, they continued believing God is the only true God.

When the king's statue was built, he commanded everyone to bow down when the music started. Everyone did, except Shadrach, Meshach and Abednego. Some people were already upset with the Jews, and the boys' refusal to bow down added salt to the wound and made for good information to be taken to the king.

The boys were highly regarded by the king, but when he learned about their refusal to bow down, they were brought in front of him. After he asked why they didn't bow and they answered, the king was angry and started seeing them differently. He even gave them an opportunity to change their minds but they refused, saying:

"King Nebuchadnezzar, we do not need to defend ourselves before you in this matter. If we are thrown into the blazing furnace, the

God we serve is able to deliver us from it, and He will deliver us from Your Majesty's hand. But even if He does not, we want you to know, Your Majesty, that we will not serve your gods or worship the image of gold you have set up."

Did you pick up on what they said in their response?

They knew God could save them and had ultimate faith, yet also accepted that even if God chose not to rescue them their response wouldn't change. Simply put, they would not bow down to an idol.

The king's anger burned within him, and he instructed his soldiers to turn up the furnace seven times hotter than normal. It was so hot that the men who were supposed to throw Shadrach, Meshach and Abednego in died when they came in contact with the heat.

After the boys were thrown in, there were four people in the fire, which King Nebuchadnezzar saw for himself. The fourth man appeared like a son of God.

Later, Shadrach, Meshach and Abednego walked around without being harmed. Nothing on them was singed, except the cords which with they were bound.

Do you know what the King's response was when he instructed their release from the furnace?

He said, "Praise be to the God of Shadrach, Meshach and Abednego, who has sent his angel and rescued his servants! They trusted in him and defied the king's command and were willing to give up their lives rather than serve or worship any god except their own God. Therefore, I decree that the people of any nation or language who say anything against the God of Shadrach, Meshach and Abednego be cut into pieces and their houses be turned into piles of rubble, for no other god can save in this way.""

Because the three Hebrew boys stood their ground, the king witnessed the power of God and what He can do. So much so that no one was allowed to talk against the Most High God thereafter. The chapter ended with Shadrach, Meshach and Abednego being promoted.

Let us stand for what we believe in, no matter the cost.

Dear Heavenly Father, thank you for these lessons. Lord,

give us wisdom as we open Your word that we may read the same stories with a new understanding. Help us to stand our ground in our beliefs.

Be still before the LORD and wait patiently for him; do not fret when people succeed in their ways, when they carry out their wicked schemes.

PSALM 37:7 NIV

Thought to ponder

Have you ever been in a situation that you had to stand up for what you believed, no matter the cost? What was the end result?

DAY 44

Negative Self-Talk

In the last day or so, I've heard my five-year old starting to speak negatively over herself.

Once we were in the car and she started fussing over something and I told her no. Not in an angry way, but no just the same. She started crying and saying, "I'm a horrible person." Huh? Where did that come from, I wondered.

She's since done that a few times in the last twenty-four hours with some version of "I can't do anything right." Again, I wondered, Say what? Where is this negative talk coming from? While I thought it was just a phase, I took it seriously.

I don't speak negatively over her or myself, and I'm careful to teach her that it's not ok to talk that way. Based on scripture my pastor quoted from Jeremiah 1:5a, "before I formed you in the womb, I knew you," I reminded her that I've never told her she's a bad child or that she doesn't do things right.

Sadly, this isn't always the case. Sometimes we grow up hearing negative things about ourselves and we internalize them and start believing the negativity we hear.

Was that your situation? As an adult, can you still hear the negative things others said about you. Do the negative things said to you as a child, by a previous significant other or spouse said about you still ring in your ears?

How do you overcome this?

You can carry God's truth in your heart and seek His promises for you. Read His word to learn what it says and how He feels about you. My Bible tells me I'm "fearfully and wonderfully made." Before I was formed, God chose me and set me apart. God, just like He did with Adam and Eve in the garden, took time to make me in His image. All the other animals were created, but He took time to take the dirt and formed us and breathe life into us.

Just in case you need this reminder today: You are loved by your Heavenly Father! You are special! He chose you before you were even born!

Dear Heavenly Father, thank you for loving us with an everlasting love. Thank you for making us in Your image, and reminding us that we are fearfully and wonderfully made. Lord, some of us have grown up hearing that we won't amount to much, please help us to know that these are untruths from people whose opinions carry no, or little, weight in our lives. And Lord, if we are the ones speaking negatively over others, please help us realize how destructive that practice can be.

Keep me as the apple of your eye; hide me in the shadow of your wings from the wicked who are out to destroy me, from my mortal enemies who surround me.

PSALM 17:8-9 NIV

Thought to ponder

How can learning specific scripture change the way you think about and tell yourself? Find 3 verses, write them down and recite them of what God says about you.

DAY 45
My Bruised Thumb

I went excavating last night.

Well. Not really. I sat in my living room and "excavated" a dinosaur from an egg.

I gave my daughter money to buy gifts for her teachers and a few family members, along with a budget on how much to spend on each person.

She came back with a gift for each of them, but spent the most money on herself though her name wasn't on the list.

The item she chose for herself was a dinosaur egg, with excavating tools including a plastic pick and brush. The job of excavating it out was left to us. I told her I'd help her, but we'd have to make time to get it done. When you tell that to a then five-year-old, be prepared to get asked every five minutes if it's time yet. (Hmmm. That kind of sounds like me when I'm asking God for something.)

After she chiseled for a few minutes, she'd barely scratched the surface. I knew it was going to take more energy and strength than she had, so I took over.

I chiseled and brushed for what seemed like a very long time, but long enough to get only the body and tail out of the egg — and acquired a sore thumb with a fully formed blister.

I showed her my now-bruised thumb and asked her if she saw just how much I was willing to do for her because I loved her so much.

In that moment, I thought of a very different kind of bruising.

I thought of Jesus' nail-scarred hands. My little blister is nothing compared to the pain Jesus endured to demonstrate His love for us. He loves us so much that we was willing to suffer on the cross for sins that He had not committed, so that we would be free from guilt and shame and have a chance at eternal life.

Do you know just how much Jesus loves you? My daughter knows I love her because I tell her about my little bruised thumb, but that pales in comparison to Jesus being born so He could sacrifice His life for us.

Dear Heavenly Father, we thank You for your love. We thank You for your willingness to die on Calvary for us to show us the depth of your love. Lord, help us to realize that we're no longer bound because you have come to set us free. Help us not to live with a mantle of shame and regret.

For God so loved the world, that he gave his only begotten Son, that whosoever believeth in him should not perish, but have everlasting life.

JOHN 3:16 KJV

Thought to ponder

Do you know just how much God really loves you?

DAY 46

Time

Are you like me, always wishing you had more time to do X, Y and Z?

For many years, I was constantly running. And when I say running, I do mean running. Running in the morning to get out of the house to take my daughter to school. Running to drop her off on time. Running out of the school so I can catch my train.

This went on for a very long time. So much so, that one of the employees at the school gently pulled me aside one day and told me that I needed to slow down.

I had prided myself on always being busy, but at some point, fortunately, I began to realize that what I was doing wasn't healthy. I also knew that God had been creating a change in my life, and it was about to take effect within a matter of weeks. I promised I would take heed and finally slow down.

After being so busy for so long, I literally had to learn how to slow down. It was a difficult change, but I adjusted and learned what worked and what didn't with my schedule.

Fast forward to about ten months later, when the whole world came to a screeching halt due to the coronavirus.

While I had learned to slow down, there were other aspects that I would now have to learn to do on the fly - just like many others around me were having to do. One of the adjustments I had to make was spending so much time with my daughter — which I'd been saying I wanted to be able to do.

Many of us, for quite some time, have needed to slow down; however, I don't think any of us imagined we would be forced to slow down by a deadly virus. Because of the coronavirus, I had to learn to readjust my expectations. The more I've learned to adjust, the better things have become and the more precious this time has become to me.

Before coronavirus, I wanted to make sure I did EVERYTHING. But now reality has set in that I'm not superhuman after all, and I'd have to choose. I've chosen to ensure that my daughter and I don't simply survive this crisis. I want us to thrive in spite of this crisis.

My daughter and I are doing things together that we never seemed to have time to do before. We were both always on the go, so there was just never enough time. Now we're able to cook together and do silly artwork that I'd frankly rather avoid because I'm not artistic – but now thoroughly enjoying the experience. We play rough and tumble together and experience a joy with each other that makes me grateful we have this time together. (Mind you. I'm not happy about what has caused us to have this time together. Please don't misunderstand what I'm saying here.)

How have you adjusted your quarantine time to ensure you remain sane and thrive?

Dear Heavenly Father, thank you for this precious time together. I know this is an extremely difficult, trying and stressful time for so many. Nevertheless, Father, I want to remain thankful for the positives that I see coming from this COVID-19 pandemic. Father, I ask that You draw us closer to You and those who are around us on a daily basis. Thank you for this time.

Teach us to number our days, that we may gain a heart of wisdom.

PSALM 90:12 NIV

Thought to ponder

What were some of your fondest memories while you were in quarantine?

DAY 47
God Can Change Your Situation in an Instant

When I moved into my new home, my dad planted three pine trees and some shrubs to beautify my front yard. My job was to plant pretty flowers and water them. As I was completely new to gardening, I did my best at watering my plants, but somehow the Pine trees still died. I don't think they had taken root properly.

Because they had been planted deep in the ground, I wasn't strong enough to pull them out myself, and so I just left them. In between the vibrant pink, purple and orange flowers I planted annually were the dead Pine trees. For some reason, I'd gotten accustomed to seeing them and they didn't bother me as much — life and death in the same garden.

It had been nearly a year since I'd told my father about my dead Pine trees, but he hadn't had time to do anything about them until today. He told me weeks ago he had new flowers for me, and we both knew pulling the Pine trees would be his job. A few days ago he'd called to say he'd be in my neck of the woods, he'd bring my plants and I didn't even need to be home.

Since I knew my father had planned to stop by, when I got home that night, one of the first things I did was rush to the front yard to see what he'd done. As I took it all in, I gushed over my father's landscaping prowess. He'd pulled up the dead Pine trees and planted more Pine and more trees than were there before. Now my pretty purple, pink and orange flowers bloomed against a vibrant backdrop of living shrubs.

What situation are you waiting for your Heavenly Father to bring to life? You've told Him of your need, but He's told you the time isn't quite right yet. He knows your need and that you're not strong enough to bring life back into your own situation.

In Ezekiel Thirty-seven, God asks Ezekiel if the dry bones could live. I love Ezekiel's response: "Lord, only You alone know." God knows all about your dry bones situation and He alone can bring it to life by adding flesh, tendons and breath. But, you must trust Him and keep having faith. He's the one who can turn your situation around at just the right moment.

> Dear Heavenly Father, we thank You for earthly fathers who can teach us. We thank You for stepping in when situations appear lifeless and, just as you resurrected an army, bringing back what we think is dead in our own lives. Help us to trust You with all our hearts and lean not unto our own understanding, as the Bible says in Proverbs 3:5.

> **4** *Then he said to me, "Prophesy to these bones and say to them, 'Dry bones, hear the word of the LORD!* **5** *This is what the Sovereign LORD says to these bones: I will make breath[a] enter you, and you will come to life.* **6** *I will attach tendons to you and make flesh come upon you and cover you with skin; I will put breath in you, and you will come to life. Then you will know that I am the LORD.'"*
>
> EZEKIEL 37:4-6 NIV

Thought to ponder

Is there a situation in your life that you are asking God to do the impossible? To bring life back to a situation that you believe is dead?

DAY 48

God vs Alexa...

I recently bought an Echo Dot, after doing very quick research before purchasing it to ascertain whether it was something I'd actually use. After a bit of hemming and hawing, I decided to get it to pair with another wireless device that I definitely needed.

An Echo Dot is a device that responds to voice instructions. After the initial set up, I started talking to Alexa, and it didn't take long for my daughter to look up in amazement and say, "Mom, she can do everything!" I had to laugh. She can't do everything, I told my daughter, adding that I wish she would clean up for me.

I love it that after I call her name she responds within seconds and tells me exactly what I need to know. Of course, being the impatient person, I am, I start thinking. Jeez, I wish God responded as quickly and clearly to my requests. Even now as I'm typing I have to laugh at myself.

I realize God does answer my prayers, and just as I'm free to ask Alexa questions anytime I want, I have the same privilege of calling on the God of the universe and asking Him any questions when I want. God may not answer the way Alexa does, but He sure answers. The question I have to ask myself is: Am I listening to what He's telling me? In Jeremiah 33:3, the Bible states, "Call to Me and I will answer you, and I will tell you great and mighty things, which you do not know." Are you calling on Him?

Do you know one of the major differences between God and Alexa? Unlike my daughter's wrong assumption that Alexa can do everything, the God that I serve CAN DO EVERYTHING. And He knows everything, too.

Dear Heavenly Father, thank you for hearing our requests, even when we don't call your name when we talk to you. Thank you, also, for hearing the unspoken words in our hearts and responding to them. Thank you for a love that encompasses all and for being able to do ALL things.

Then you will call on me and come and pray to me, and I will listen to you.

JEREMIAH 29:12 NIV

Thought to ponder

Are you calling on your Heavenly Father? Are you waiting for His response?

DAY 49

Listening to Foolish Advice

Have you ever made a decision based on bad information?

This is what happened to Haman in the book of Esther. Esther, who was described as lovely in form and feature, had earned the king's heart. Apparently, she also won what appeared to be a beauty pageant, with becoming the Queen as the prize.

Haman was already angry at Mordecai because Mordecai refused to acknowledge Haman's status. He had been stewing in his anger for some time and trying to devise ways to get rid of Mordecai and the whole Jewish population.

Haman once again passes the courts' gate, and Mordecai once again refuses to acknowledge him. Although he's in high spirits because Queen Esther invited only he and the king to a fancy feast, Haman chose to focus on fueling his anger because of Mordecai. He went home and called together his wife and friends to ask their advice on what to do about Mordecai, the Jew who refused to bow to him. This was clearly an issue about ego, but instead of telling him to drop his foolish ego, they added fuel to the fire by advising him to build a seventy-five feet high gallows and request of the king that Mordecai be hanged on it.

This idea delighted Haman, and he had the gallows built.

But God had a different plan.

We find out later that once again Haman's ego got him in trouble, ultimately causing his own humiliation and death on the gallows he'd built for Mordecai. It reminds me of what they say about pointing a finger. When you point a finger at someone, there are three fingers pointing back at you.

Whose advice are you listening to? Does their advice seem full of wisdom, or are they simply boosting your ego and telling you what you want to hear?

Dear Heavenly Father, we thank you for blessing us with friends with wisdom. Lord, help us to discern to whom we share our thoughts. Help them to council us with things that are of You, even if it's not what we want to hear. Help us to ultimately make wise decisions that will glorify You.

Walk with the wise and become wise, for a companion of fools suffers harm.

PROVERBS 13:20 NIV

Thought to ponder

What can you say about the friendships you have? Do they offer you wise council or do they tell you what you want to hear?

DAY 50

Being Loved and Seen

In the summer of 2017 I was blessed to attend a women's speaking and writing conference with 800 other women. How I even got there is a testimony all to itself which I may share one of these days.

Today, I want to share about my first hours at the conference.

I had gotten there the day before to ensure that I could settle in and have some time to unwind. It was lunch time when I arrived and registered. I went to grab my lunch in the food area. I love the sun, and there was one spot that the sun was streaming through the roof - whether unintentionally or intentionally, that is now a part of the story.

As I sat with the sun beaming down on me, quite a few women walked by me. They looked, saw, and kept going. Needless to say, I felt like the first day of a new school - except I was well into my 30s.

But Jennifer came. She was with another friend, and she chose to sit with me. She looked at me, and her exact words were, 'I bet you've been passed over because you're in the sun, but I'm going to sit with you'. After we introduced ourselves, it turned out her daughter and I shared first names, with a different spelling.

In that moment, Jennifer, not knowing it, showed me such love and kindness. She showed me what it looked like to be truly seen in a room of so many. In a recent conversation with her, which I saved because it was just so beautiful, she explained that what she saw was God pouring His sunlight on me, and that she was wise enough to see it. Needless to say, she had me crying buckets.

Jennifer did not know it at the time, but I thanked God for her as I wrote in my journal that first night. And because of her, the very next morning I returned her kindness to multiple other women, and also gained another friend because she felt seen and loved in my presence. We are still friends to this day.

How can you show up for those who may feel unseen in our society? When I grow up, I want to be just like Jennifer, sharing love and kindness to those I come in contact with.

Dear Heavenly Father, thank you for friends who make us feel seen when we feel unseen. Thank you that your love truly reaches down to the depths of who we are, and sometimes that will come in the form of another human. Please show us how to extend grace and love to those we come in contact with.

The King will reply, 'Truly I tell you, whatever you did for one of the least of these brothers and sisters of mine, you did for me.'

MATTHEW 25:40 NIV

Thought to ponder

Is there someone who comes to mind that you can show love and kindness – even though they might be difficult to love?

DAY 51

Are You in Deep Waters?

I lost my brother thirteen years ago.

He tragically drowned though he was an excellent swimmer, and was much better than me. While I've always loved the water, his passing created an apprehension in me about putting my face in the water when I swim. To be honest, in the months following his drowning, I couldn't even put my face directly in line of the shower spray.

Recently, something remarkable happened to me. I'd been invited to my friend's pool and though I'd swam in it before, I'd really kept to the edge. I was a relatively good swimmer and know how to float and tread water. But since I lost my brother, I've stayed away from deep waters. If my feet couldn't touch the bottom, I had no interest in being there. While we were at the pool, one of the girls handed me her face mask, which was full and covered my eyes and nose. Although I hated the feeling of my nose being restricted, I took a few breaths through my mouth and fought the panic. My friend, a good swimmer, was there, so I knew I'd be able to get back to the edge of the pool relatively easily if I needed to.

Something shifted, and I was able to do something I hadn't been able to do in ten years: relax, breathe and swim in the deep waters. It was a feeling of exhilaration, and I swam across the pool in the deep end back and forth at least ten times.

As I've thought of those moments since yesterday, a passage keeps coming to mind, "When you pass through the waters, I will be with you; and when you pass through the rivers, they will not sweep over you."

I pray whatever situation you're facing right now - especially if you feel like you're swimming in deep waters, - will be eased with the comfort that comes from knowing of God's promise to be right there with you.

Dear Heavenly Father, thank you for promising to be with us. Help us to be bold and to hold onto Your promises.

When you pass through the waters, I will be with you; and when you pass through the rivers, they will not sweep over you.

ISAIAH 43:2A NIV

Thought to ponder

If you are going through a difficult or terrifying situation at the moment, how can you hold on to God's unchanging hands to gain His strength?

DAY 52

Connecting to Jesus

I am without a phone today.

When I got to the train platform, I started looking in my bag and realized I didn't have it. As I sat on the train, I absent-mindedly reached for my phone because it's the perfect time to catch up on news, text my friends or go on social media sites. I guess my reaching for the phone was similar to knowing the power is out in your home yet instinctively flicking the light switch on as soon as you walk in the door. You flick the switch, but you're still in the dark. I reached for my phone, but it still wasn't there, so I closed my eyes and slept.

When I got off the train, I panicked. How was I going to order my morning drink? I typically order it about five minutes prior to getting to the store, then waltz right in, grab my drink and waltz right back out without waiting. Then I remembered I still had my wallet with my trusty credit card.

As soon as I got to work, I asked a colleague to use the find my iPhone" app to locate my device, and sure enough it was at home where I'd left it. I was thankful I hadn't lost it.

Minutes later I went to log into my bank account, but I couldn't because the system needed to send me an email or text so I could verify my identity -- both of which I needed to use my phone.

All of these events really made me start thinking.

Imagine if I were this connected to Jesus? As I recounted all of the things for which I needed my phone, I realize just how attached I am to it. I want to get to the point that for everything I need, I reach out to Jesus or my Bible for the answers.

Dear Heavenly Father, thank you for your lessons from such simple things. Lord, help us to stay connected to you because if not, we will lack strength and be unable to grow into the people You have called us to be. Help us to use our time wisely so that we will be able to build deeper and stronger roots in You.

*I am the vine; you are the branches. If you remain in me and I in you, you will bear much fruit; apart from me you can do nothing. **6** If you do not remain in me, you are like a branch that is thrown away and withers; such branches are picked up, thrown into the fire and burned. **7** If you remain in me and my words remain in you, ask whatever you wish, and it will be done for you. **8** This is to my Father's glory, that you bear much fruit, showing yourselves to be my disciples.*

JOHN 15:5-8 NIV

Thought to ponder

How can you remain even more connected to the Vine than you are to a cell phone?

DAY 53

Wisdom

Do you have a favorite "wisdom" story in the Bible?

My all-time favorite has to be when King Solomon thought he was in a dream when God asked Solomon what he wanted from Him.

Instead of Solomon asking for riches or longevity or any of those things one might typically request, he asked for wisdom from God to rule God's people. You see, Solomon was around the age of twenty when he took his father's place on the throne, and he knew what he didn't know. So, he asked God for Divine wisdom.

Because it was such a sincere, heartfelt request, God granted it.

Proverbs 4:7 NIV states: "The beginning of wisdom is this: Get wisdom. Though it cost all you have, get understanding."

People came from all over to hear Solomon speak and render judgment. They knew without a doubt that his wisdom came from God.

There is another story that jumps out at me that demonstrates how godly wisdom was executed.

It is the story of Moses' mother. Pharaoh had proclaimed that all of the little boys should be killed. Moses' mother knew that he was special and so she hid him for three months. When she couldn't hide him any longer, she made a secure basket, put him in it and pushed it in the water in the direction of Pharaoh's daughter who was bathing. In addition, to ensure that her precious baby boy was safe, she sent his sister Miriam to watch the basket.

When Pharaoh's daughter found the basket, Miriam appeared and offered to find a nurse for him. Unbeknownst to Pharaoh's daughter, the nurse was the baby's mother.

Moses was supposed to be killed as a child, but instead he was raised by his own mother in the presence of Pharaoh and his daughter, which in turn prepared him for his ultimate role of freeing the Israelites many years later.

Gosh, there are so many lessons here, apart from executing godly wisdom. As I'm writing this, I'm reminded that God used Moses' time in the palace and later in the desert as time of preparation. He would need multiple skill sets to relate to Pharaoh and to lead the Israelites through the desert for forty years.

I'm learning that I have to pray for wisdom constantly for all of the decisions I have to make.

Friends, I invite you to pray as well. God hears and answers in remarkable ways.

> Dear Heavenly Father, thank you for godly wisdom. Help us to use the wisdom and understanding we gain to do Your work and to further Your kingdom. Help us to be kind to one other.

> *The beginning of wisdom is this: Get wisdom. Though it cost all you have, get understanding.*
>
> PROVERBS 4:7 NIV

Thought to ponder

How have you seen God answer your request for wisdom? If you've never asked, would you try doing so now?

DAY 54

What You Need, Where and When You Need It.

Have you been praying a specific request and seemingly nothing is happening? That's how I felt right before this devotion. I had been praying specifically on a topic to share with my audience.

I ran out to get my lunch and saw the following on the side of a truck — "What you need. Where and when you need it." Isn't that exactly how God provides? So, I want to share a bit with you of how I see God providing. I've also come to realize that He doesn't provide only physical or material needs but spiritual ones as well.

I went to a women's speaking and writing conference over the weekend and was in awe over seeing eight hundred women who felt called to ministry in different aspects in the same room. The worship experience was unbelievable, almost like nothing I've ever experienced. Many of us were either on a speaking, writing or combination track, and some of us, like me, were there because of obedience and because God had opened the door for us. Initially, some of us weren't even sure about attending, but we knew God had led us there so we were there. Isn't that like God to call you and say, "I know you're not ready, but I'm calling, come as you are!?"As I said, it was just beautiful.

At some point closer to the end of the conference, I felt like God had revealed to me what He wants from me. And let me tell you, sometimes what God wants for us isn't necessarily what we want for ourselves. However, after really letting myself be still, I finally heard the calling that I think my writing and sharing have been preparing me for -- one that I've avoided for as many years as I've been around. It's fair to say that my experiences have molded me and helped me grow.

It wasn't until I was at the airport, ready to come home, that I really accepted what God was asking of me. I had learned while at the conference that He wants me to focus on ministry in my home church. In fact, I think I'm being led to the Single Parent Ministry in my home church. No sooner than I'd admitted that out loud to a dear friend, I saw another woman who had attended the same conference. I hadn't had the opportunity to speak with her as our paths hadn't crossed, but when we started talking she shared what she was passionate about and where God had been leading her. Do you want to take a guess as to one of the areas she'd focused on? Yup, Single Parent Ministry in her home church, plus sharing with others.

I met many wonderful women at the conference, but I think God waited to introduce me to her because by then I'd realize only He could provide me with the resources to accomplish what He's asking of me. And believe it or not, although there were women from all over the country at the conference, she lives in New York, maybe a half hour away from me.

What is God asking of you? Have you been reluctant to say yes because of a fear that you don't know what to do or believe you're not good enough to do it? I'm learning that if God is calling you to do something, He will equip you and give you the resources to accomplish the task He's set before you.

Dear Heavenly Father, help us to walk boldly in our calling. Help us not to cower in fear of the unknown or in self-doubt — especially when You are calling us. God, we know that You will provide what we need, when and where we need it.

The LORD makes firm the steps of the one who delights in him; 24 though he may stumble, he will not fall, for the LORD upholds him with his hand.

PSALM 37 23-24 NIV

Thought to ponder

Is there a direction that you feel like God is calling you in, but it does not quite make sense? How can you confirm this?

DAY 55

Keep Pressing On

Ishared about this before – doing what you are doing, even if you think no one is noticing. I have another clear example that jumped out at me in my devotion yesterday. As I was reading through the second chapter in Ruth, after having read a novel on her character recently, I noticed something about her.

Ruth had left her hometown to remain with her mother-in-law, even though she didn't know what her future held. She knew two things: She was going with Naomi, and she was determined to trust God with her situation – even though as a Moabite she would likely have grown up worshipping idols. She made a conscious decision with Naomi when she stated, "Your God [will be] my God" Ruth 1:16b.

Ruth did everything she could to make Naomi's life comfortable. I don't think she was looking for recognition; she was looking to fulfill her promise to take care of Naomi in her older years. She went willingly to the fields to glean, even being the one to proactively ask Naomi what the customs were for those who were poor. She went with Naomi's permission and blessing.

When Boaz met her, her reputation had long preceded her. While she may have been fulfilling her promises to Naomi, others recognized what she had been doing for Naomi, especially because she was a stranger in a foreign land.

My appeal to you will likely be similar to the last time. Are you doing something but feel like you're getting nowhere? Don't give up. As long as you're doing what you think you've been called to do, God sees your efforts and will reward them when the time is right.

Dear Heavenly Father, thank you for your Biblical teachings and examples of how we should live. Lord, sometimes it's difficult to keep doing without seeing the rewards, but we know we must continue doing whatever work You've called us to do. Help us to realize that Your timing is more perfect than any we can ever imagine, and to continue trusting You in all circumstances.

Being confident of this, that he who began a good work in you will carry it on to completion until the day of Christ Jesus.

PHILIPPIANS 1:6 NLT

Thought to ponder

What do you feel like you have been doing consistently but not getting the desired results? Do you need to reassess or do you need to continue doing what you are doing?

DAY 56

God's Promises

There are times when I feel stuck and even after praying about it, just don't know what to write.

That's when I open my Bible and become even more intentional. I can't give up, because I've made a promise to God and He's made a promise to me. You see, I've had to be intentional about how I look for God's hands in my life to share what God is doing. Sometimes it pops up pretty easily, and sometimes I have to do a little digging.

Today is one of those digging days.

I opened my Bible knowing in my heart that I needed a topic and landed on Isaiah 61. As I read it, my breathing relaxed and I smiled. It has such powerful imagery of God making promises to His people. The passage which was written by the prophet Isaiah speaks of God's unfailing love. The topic of this passage in my bible is "The Year of the Lord's Favor." Isaiah 61:2-3 NIV states "to proclaim the year of the Lord's favor and the day of vengeance of our God, to comfort all who mourn, and provide for those who grieve in Zion — to bestow on them a crown of beauty instead of ashes, the oil of gladness instead of mourning, and a garment of praise instead of a spirit of despair. They will be called oaks of righteousness, a planting of the Lord for the display of his splendor."

I'm smiling all over again, after reading and typing those verses. You might be going through a difficult season in your life right now, but what promises! And I know from my personal experience that when God promises something, He fulfills them.

Friends, let us cling to His promises to make beauty from our ashes and replace the crown of ashes (shame and despair) with a crown of beauty.

> Dear Heavenly Father, we thank you for making all things new. Help us to seek You first in everything we do. Help us to cling to Your promises and help us to hold on just a little while longer. Teach us how to be faithful to You.

> *The LORD himself goes before you and will be with you; he will never leave you nor forsake you. Do not be afraid; do not be discouraged.*
> DEUTERONOMY 31:8 NIV

Thought to ponder

Have you ever experienced God's promises first hand? If not, will you ask God to do something specific in your life that only He can answer?

DAY 57

Just Do It!

Today's title sounds like the Nike ad slogan, but it's actually an encouragement to you and me to just do what God has placed on our hearts!

Today is a special day. It is my mother's birthday, and I gladly and lovingly celebrate her, but it's also the four-year anniversary of my blog, which was started on this date to honor mom for all she's done.

My first post four years ago was titled "I'm ready, well maybe!" You see, had I left it up to me, I think I'd still be sitting at my desk trying to figure out how to create a blog. Fortunately for me, God saw fit to work out the mechanics. On my own, I'd still be debating whether I have what it takes to write anything, much less something that would interest others. Thankfully God said to leave the words and topics to Him. You see, had someone told me I'd be in this position four years later, I would have said stop making up stories. But God said, "I can see the beginning from the end, but you MUST trust me." So, four years ago, I officially started out on a Faith Journey.

And God, I thank you for helping me along this highway and making the journey just a little bit easier.

Just last night I commented on a friend's Instagram post. I awakened to a response from her that she's still working on her "faith muscles." Her words reminded me of one of my first blogs, in which I shared how God strengthens us by using the example of my then-thirty-three-pound daughter. Thank God she didn't grow to be thirty-three pounds overnight, or I wouldn't have been able to carry her. Instead, God in his infinite wisdom allowed her to grow a little at a time from her original birth weight of three pounds, four ounces. So it is with us. God gives us little things each time so that He may increase our faith. I can see that after about three hundred blog posts over the course of the last four years, God strengthened me and reminded me that this is not about me, but instead it's about my obedience to whatever He's asking of me.

What is God asking you to do? What is God asking you to release to Him so He can work in your life? Whatever it is, just do it! God is able to do immeasurably more than we can ever think of asking Him, but we must trust Him and His process. His way of getting you to the destination may not be the way you had in mind, but God can see through all of the congestion and construction ahead that you can't see. He might take you on many detours but the key is not to lose hope or faith.

> Dear Heavenly Father, I come to You with nothing but a broken, contrite heart, asking You to do what only You can do. Please open our eyes to see You and your immense love for us. Please help us to accept that You won't allow anything to happen without purpose. Continue teaching us Your ways, because Your ways are higher and better than any we can imagine. Allow us to let go of anything that is unlike you.

> *And we know that in all things God works for the good of those who love him, who have been called according to his purpose.*
>
> ROMANS 8:28 NIV

Thought to ponder

If you have been reluctant to do what God is calling you to do, how can you take the first step? I promise, you do not need to see the whole staircase. This is exercising faith.

DAY 58
Being Present For Each Other

I saw a post on social media that prompted other people to share. A very popular Instagram figure shared her heart through poetry, touching hundreds of thousands of people around the world. (That can be one of the positive aspects of social media.) The author's writing is helping to heal a lot of past hurts because of her candidness and the messages of peace and love she espouses. She shared a message that she received, and shortly thereafter shared another very similar one that someone else shared as encouragement.

You see, social media is a community. It can be used for positivity as well as negativity, for good as well as bad. In this case, there's a woman who's offering to help another woman from a different part of the world heal — all because one was brave enough to open up about her struggles.

I think that's what God wants of us, to help each other. Just like iron sharpens iron, so, too, are we called to show and extend love to others. We don't need to be next-door neighbors, especially with social media. But we do need to be open to allowing the Holy Spirit to lead in our lives and help us to realize when others need us.

I heard someone say we've become so busy staring at our phones that we're missing the very people we've been called to minister. I know I'm guilty of that at times.

I want to be more aware of my surroundings to ensure I don't miss that one person God has placed in my path to bless. That may require slowing down the pace of my life and listening to Him. When we get busy, we have a tendency to rush and not spend time in His presence. It's only through constant communication that we will hear His voice.

Dear Heavenly Father, please help us to slow down and to listen to You. Help us not to be so busy that we miss the people You've placed in front of us for us to minister to. And Lord, soften our hearts so that we don't misjudge situations based on our preconceived notions. Speak to our hearts and convict us of the work You would have us do.

Be completely humble and gentle; be patient, bearing with one another in love.

EPHESIANS 4:2 NIV

Thought to ponder

How can you share what God has been doing in your life so that you can help someone else overcome what they have gone through?

DAY 59

Letting Go Of What Holds Us Back

Now that the weather is finally warming up, I like to take my daughter to the park. It feels like we've been cooped up all winter and our goal is to make the best of every moment of the nicer weather.

We recently found a new park (new to us) in our neighborhood that provides some pretty neat activities. There's one activity that I've never seen at any of the other park. It consists of three, separate platforms held firmly by a bar at the top and anchored by chains on the bottom, making it moveable. To get across to the next platform, you have to step widely enough or bring two of the platforms close enough to each other.

The first time we went, my daughter was fascinated by the contraption after watching a child playing on it. She tried to master it multiple times but gave up out of fear that she'd fall. It's secure, but it feels wobbly as people struggle to move across it. I kept reminding her that I was standing right next to her and I would help her go from one platform to the other, and most importantly, I wouldn't let her fall. It took her a full hour to build up the courage and confidence to get across once. But even after one time, she felt accomplished.

Fast forward to exactly a week later. I decided to surprise her with another trip to this park. As usual, she was excited. Almost as soon as we got there, she headed straight for this particular activity. She knew I'd be standing there and supporting her way across. On this day she made it across successfully not once, but at least six times in twenty minutes!

You see, I knew I wanted to share this with you when it happened the first time. But the lesson was even more powerful because I waited to share after witnessing it a second time.

Sometimes we're so fearful of letting go of what's holding us back, which, of course, keeps us from moving forward. My daughter learned that she couldn't keep holding onto the firm anchor of the other part of the jungle gym if she wanted to make it across each of the moving platforms. But she also knew I was going to be right there, and as her mom, my job was to protect her from falling.

Is there something in your life that has you firmly anchored to the past and the safety that it provides? It may feel safe, but I know God wants you to keep moving forward. He has promised that He'll catch us, but we do have to trust Him. What is God asking of you? You have to trust that He's able to protect you and not let you fall.

Dear Heavenly Father, thank you for Your love and protection and for all You do. Help us to trust You and to grow each day in our relationship with You, knowing that You will not allow us to fall if we keep trusting You.

Brothers and sisters, I do not consider myself yet to have taken hold of it. But one thing I do: Forgetting what is behind and straining toward what is ahead, I press on toward the goal to win the prize for which God has called me heavenward in Christ Jesus.

PHILIPPIANS 3:13-14 NIV

Thought to ponder

How can you let go of the former things (your past) so that you can move forward into what God has in store for you?

DAY 60

Step Out of the Boat of Comfort

*If you don't step out of the boat,
you will never walk on water.*

Mark Batterson
Draw the Circle: 40 Day Prayer Challenge

In the last few years, I've stepped out of many things that once held my comfort. I've done many things but realize I don't grow much in my comfort zone.

The more I've taken one step of obedience, the more God has trusted me to do the next thing.

It started with a simple act of obedience of writing, which didn't make sense as I'm not a writer. Then it moved into speaking and even publishing a book. Now, you are reading the end of my second book.

If you think that's crazy to you, it's even crazier to me.

After those initial steps of obedience, I was given the green light to leave a secure job that had taken care of all my needs and many of my wants. It had taught me so much and helped mold me into who I'd become. But my time there was done, and God opened a new door of entrepreneurship. It seemed crazy, but because of my previous steps of obedience, God now trusted me with this step. And in turn, I also trusted God because I have witnessed first hand that He does not steer me wrong.

In the first eight months, while in the process of growing a business, I've been able to do so much and to meet many wonderful people.

But that would not have happened had I not stepped out of my boat of comfort.

What boat of comfort are you staying safely in when God is asking you to step out and walk on water? Trust Him. It may not be easy, but I promise you won't be disappointed. Just keep taking each step of obedience, one step at a time.

Dear Heavenly Father, thank you for seeing everything long before it's even a thought in our minds. Help us to walk in obedience for each step You'd have us take, even when the next step seems scary or unknown. After all, you already know the plans for us.

11 For I know the plans I have for you," declares the LORD, "plans to prosper you and not to harm you, plans to give you hope and a future. 12 Then you will call on me and come and pray to me, and I will listen to you.

JEREMIAH 29:11-12 NIV

Thought to ponder

After reading these devotions, what are some of the steps of obedience you believe God is calling you towards? Write them down, and ask God how to move forward.

Acknowledgements

There are so many who have encouraged me along the way as I have endeavored to write this book. To say it's been an incredible journey is an understatement.

First, I want to thank my friend, Michael Charles, and his lovely wife, Johan. Michael planted the seed that I should write. He believed I had a story to share. I laughed at him and told him I was not a writer. He kept planting the seeds. Later, when my friend, Stuart Williams, suggested I write, I took note. He watered the seeds that Michael had planted. I had just started journaling and sharing my heart with God, but Stuart's suggestion seemed to come out of left field as he would not have known that. After a very short time, it was confirmed that I was supposed to start writing. What a crazy thought, yet now I've written a second book.

But God...

I want to thank my Mom, Marcia Grant, for being my rock and being so supportive of all of my endeavors — even the ones that don't always make sense initially. I'd also like to thank my spiritual Mom, Marcia Hamilton, and her beautiful family. That's right. I'm blessed to have two Marcias who both mother and love me. I would be remiss if I didn't thank my dad, Hector Roberts, the best dad in the world and a man who is always there when I need him – even now that I'm an adult with a child of my own. I must also thank my amazing Amelia, who continues to surprise me with her level of wisdom, understanding and generosity.

I must also thank my friend, David Francis, an amazing photographer who has taken my professional shots, including those used on both back covers of my books and the ones I use for my speaking engagements.

Now I must thank Roxann Stephens and Tamika Bucknor, who have walked the crazy faith journey with me from the beginning. They haven't told me how nuts my thoughts are, but instead have stayed by my side and encouraged me. Thanks to my friend Crystal E. Ward, who Michael Charles insisted that I meet. He was not wrong. God truly blessed me with Crystal's friendship, in both a personal and professional capacity.

Thank you to the Mitchell and Harris/Salmon Families who have shown their support and love along the way.

I couldn't end my acknowledgements without thanking my friend Paula Sanders Blackwell, whose name, alone, seems to open doors for me. She has gone above and beyond throughout our friendship and even took time to show me how to print a label to sell books for my first book. She has shared her resources with me from the beginning, including her editor Laurie D. Willis of Laurie's Write Touch!, and even her friend Angela Henry, who has now become my mentor on my entrepreneurship journey. THANK YOU!

I am beyond thankful for my friends and family who showed up and encouraged me when I had no idea what I was supposed to be doing. They just kept right on encouraging me to keep pressing on. For those people who suggested that I write a book the first time, even though again, to me that was such a crazy thought, I thank you for planting those seeds in me and, like good horticulturists, watering them.

Many thanks to my publisher, Athena C. Shack, and her team at Watersprings Media House, LLC. She had a vision the first time and ran with it, and it was really more than I could have asked for.

This year I lost my grandfather, Birnham "Babs" Roberts, to COVID 19. I would like to honor his life with this book. I pray he rests in peace, and I pray, sincerely, that this book in some way blesses each person who reads it.

And last but certainly not least, I must acknowledge God, for without Him, none of this would have been possible.

About the Author

KAYSIAN GORDON is a mother, financial advisor, author, writer, speaker and bible teacher.

After years of education in the financial arena, Kaysian felt the call to start writing a faith blog, which she shares on her website www.kaysigordon.com and on social media. She also guest blogs for Devotable, a devotional app and website, along with the Recraft Devotional Group, a group dedicated to recrafting lives. Her writing has also been published in the North American Division of Seventh Day Adventists Women's Devotional and two Devotable compilation devotional projects.

She has taught her church's youth class and speaks to various women's groups around the country.

Kaysian has felt the call to share with others the lessons that God has been teaching her. It's in these lessons of God's faithfulness that she has stepped out of her comfort zone and is sharing the lessons that God is teaching her through everyday life situations, and living out Hebrews 11:1 NIV "Now faith is confidence in what we hope for and assurance about what we do not see."

If you'd like to connect with her regarding her blog, please email her at **kaysi@kaysigordon.com.**

www.ingramcontent.com/pod-product-compliance
Lightning Source LLC
Chambersburg PA
CBHW051112050726

47592CB00002B/791